'S[...] [...] [...] he
ex[...] [...] [...] eal
her surprise. Trying to ignore the
waves of awareness washing over
her, she took a fresh look at the man
towering over her. He still looked
m[...]e like a disreputable pirate than
[...]ernational polo player. Bracing
[...]lf, she extended her hand in
[...]ting—which he ignored and
[...]ed away.

[...]go Acosta wasn't sophisticated and he
[...]n't charming. He certainly wasn't her usual
[...]ding contact, most of whom looked to
[...]e for guidance. The thought of this man
[...]king to anyone for direction was a joke.
[...]go Acosta was a glowering tyrant who
ex[...]ected to be obeyed.

But she had dealt with difficult characters
in the past, Maxie reminded herself. It
was inevitable that she met a wide mix of
personalities during the course of her work.
Diplomacy [...] an essential part of her skill
se[...] and she [...] having
gr[...]wn up u[...]er. She
h[...] learned [...] illness
h[...] so cruel[...] [...]ow she
must learn how to manage [...].

Susan Stephens was a professional singer before meeting her husband on the tiny Mediterranean island of Malta. In true Modern™ Romance style they met on Monday, became engaged on Friday, and were married three months after that. Almost thirty years and three children later, they are still in love. (Susan does not advise her children to return home one day with a similar story, as she may not take the news with the same fortitude as her own mother!)

Susan had written several non-fiction books when fate took a hand. At a charity costume ball there was an after-dinner auction. One of the lots, 'Spend a Day with an Author', had been donated by Mills & Boon® author Penny Jordan. Susan's husband bought this lot, and Penny was to become not just a great friend but a wonderful mentor, who encouraged Susan to write romance.

Susan loves her family, her pets, her friends and her writing. She enjoys entertaining, travel, and going to the theatre. She reads, cooks, and plays the piano to relax, and can occasionally be found throwing herself off mountains on a pair of skis or galloping through the countryside. Visit Susan's website: www.susanstephens.net—she loves to hear from her readers all around the world!

Recent titles by the same author:

THE SHAMELESS LIFE OF RUIZ ACOSTA
THE UNTAMED ARGENTINIAN
RUTHLESS BOSS, DREAM BABY
  (Men Without Mercy)

Did you know these are also available as eBooks?
Visit www.millsandboon.co.uk

THE ARGENTINIAN'S SOLACE

BY
SUSAN STEPHENS

MILLS & BOON

DID YOU PURCHASE THIS BOOK WITHOUT A COVER?

If you did, you should be aware it is **stolen property** as it was reported unsold and destroyed by a retailer. Neither the author nor the publisher has received any payment for this book.

All the characters in this book have no existence outside the imagination of the author, and have no relation whatsoever to anyone bearing the same name or names. They are not even distantly inspired by any individual known or unknown to the author, and all the incidents are pure invention.

All Rights Reserved including the right of reproduction in whole or in part in any form. This edition is published by arrangement with Harlequin Enterprises II BV/S.à.r.l. The text of this publication or any part thereof may not be reproduced or transmitted in any form or by any means, electronic or mechanical, including photocopying, recording, storage in an information retrieval system, or otherwise, without the written permission of the publisher.

This book is sold subject to the condition that it shall not, by way of trade or otherwise, be lent, resold, hired out or otherwise circulated without the prior consent of the publisher in any form of binding or cover other than that in which it is published and without a similar condition including this condition being imposed on the subsequent purchaser.

® and TM are trademarks owned and used by the trademark owner and/or its licensee. Trademarks marked with ® are registered with the United Kingdom Patent Office and/or the Office for Harmonisation in the Internal Market and in other countries.

First published in Great Britain 2012
by Mills & Boon, an imprint of Harlequin (UK) Limited.
Harlequin (UK) Limited, Eton House, 18-24 Paradise Road,
Richmond, Surrey TW9 1SR

© Susan Stephens 2012

ISBN: 978 0 263 89050 1

Harlequin (UK) policy is to use papers that are natural, renewable and recyclable products and made from wood grown in sustainable forests. The logging and manufacturing process conform to the legal environmental regulations of the country of origin.

Printed and bound in Spain
by Blackprint CPI, Barcelona

THE ARGENTINIAN'S SOLACE

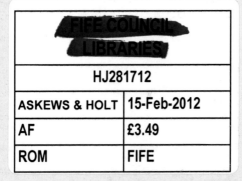

FIFE COUNCIL LIBRARIES	
HJ281712	
ASKEWS & HOLT	15-Feb-2012
AF	£3.49
ROM	FIFE

For Carly.
Intuition tells me to be excited about my new editor.

CHAPTER ONE

SHE had to close her mind to the man on the shore. Getting the old boat safely into its berth was more important. But he was like an elemental force, his gaze fixed and unswerving, with the most magnificent physique Maxie had ever seen. Tall, ripped and tanned, with wild black hair and dangerous eyes. A gold earring glinted in what light there was. Low-slung jeans over a flat, muscular belly were enough to throw anyone off course...

So think of the snarling face that would stop a rhino in its track and your concentration will come flooding back.

She had sailed the boat this far and she wasn't turning back now.

Bringing the trawler through mountainous waves single-handed had been nothing short of a miracle. They had barely made it out of the harbour when the skipper had declared himself out of action after consuming the greater part of a bottle of Scotland's finest. Maxie would be the first to admit her qualifications for sailing a boat this size were slim. She had once helped to crew a sixty-eight footer, but this old rust-bucket was proving rather more cantankerous. And she was more than a bit rusty, Maxie accepted as the deck lurched beneath her feet.

Glancing at the man on the dock, she guessed he was

waiting for her to fail. His massive forearms were crossed over his formidable chest, and his black eyes blazed with mockery and scorn.

'Welcome to Isla del Fuego,' Maxie muttered beneath her breath. But, however unfriendly the welcoming committee, she was going to berth this bucketing monster if it killed her!

Which it probably would, Maxie registered with panic as the ancient fishing craft crashed into the dock.

With relief she saw the elderly skipper had made it out of his bunk in time to take the wheel. Boiling black storm clouds suggested the weather wasn't about to change any time soon, which for a wedding planner on a scouting trip for an excited bride was somewhere south of perfect. And if the man onshore worked for the Acostas, who owned the island, he would need some serious retraining in the art of welcoming guests before the wedding, Maxie concluded, trying not to look at his glowering face.

She could always tell Holly the island was unsuitable...

The idea flitted across her mind, but it wasn't an option. She'd seen Scottish castles in worse settings transformed into fairytale palaces on a warm spring day, and damp French *châteaux* revealed in all their ancient glory when the sun shone. Plus, she trusted Holly. The bride was a smart girl, and June was a famously fabulous month in which to get married. Bottom line? If Holly wanted to get married on Isla del Fuego then it was up to Maxie to make it happen and the man on shore would just have to suck it up.

Dios! What had the storm washed in? Some pin-thin, drooping violet with—

With a very accurate and surprisingly powerful throw,

Diego conceded as he caught the rope the girl tossed him. But she had no business sailing Fernando's fishing boat—let alone slamming into the dock, thanks to her poor reading of the weather. She was lucky to be alive after sailing to the island in a storm.

'Are you ready?' she called, preparing to toss a second rope.

With his stiff leg he could only move at half her speed. The second she turned her back he limped as fast as he could to get into position before she could see him lurching like a drunk.

'Here it comes,' she warned him, in a voice that was both light and musical, yet which somehow crested the howl of the wind.

Catching the rope, he secured it. It appeared fate had a sense of humour, sending an attractive girl to the island when he could least handle the action. Resentment swept over him as he watched her darting nimbly about the deck. When his brother's fiancée had called to warn him the wedding planner was on her way he had accepted his self-imposed exile was over, but to have some lithe young girl call time was insulting. He had come down to the dock to meet the principal of the events company— someone older and sophisticated, with a keen sense of style—not some kid in jeans and a hooded top with long dark hair hanging in sodden straggles down her back. Was his brother's wedding of so little importance they'd sent some underling?

'Well caught!' she yelled, having fired another rope at him.

Well caught? There had been a time when nothing physical had been beyond him, but then his horse had rolled on him during a polo match, shattering the bones in his leg. It had been pinned in half a dozen places. He had been back on a horse and training rigorously, but it was more than a year since the accident and he had yet to regain the subtleties of sensation required for the top class game, leaving his future in polo uncertain.

'No harm done,' the girl yelled as she leaned over the rail to check the hull for damage.

'It could have been a costly mistake,' he roared back. 'You've been lucky this time.'

'Lucky?' She laughed.

He felt a surge of interest, but in his current state that was soon snuffed out. She could take a look around the island and report back to Holly, but the moment the wind dropped she was history.

No one had said planning a wedding on a remote island would be easy, Maxie reasoned, dashing spray out of her eyes. And time was of the essence, the bride had insisted. No wonder, Maxie had thought when she'd seen a photo of the groom. She had always known organising a high-profile event on a tiny island would be fraught with difficulties, but she hadn't bargained on being met by a man who made her heart beat nineteen to the dozen. She had always loved a challenge, but as a scholarship girl at an upscale school, with a home life that could best be described as chaotic, she'd made a choice early in life to remain safe on the outside looking in while other people enjoyed the arrangements she made for them.

Safe? Pulling back from the rail, she took a few steadying breaths before preparing to disembark. Nothing was safe here—especially the hard-eyed man on shore.

'Watch your step,' he barked as she started her perilous crossing of the narrow plank.

'I will,' she called back tensely, wondering why he didn't come to help her if he was so concerned.

Oh, stop fussing. She could manage. She was fine. This commission was every wedding planner's dream, and she had no intention of starting out by falling in the sea. A big society wedding between Ruiz Acosta, a fabulously wealthy Argentinian polo player, and Holly Valiant, a celebrity agony aunt who had made her name by writing a column based on living with Ruiz, would have readers hanging on Holly's every word. Having tamed the playboy, Holly was about to marry him—and the world was waiting with bated breath to see the wedding. A wedding Maxie was going to arrange. It was a commission that would take her business to the next level, and as her income supported everything she cared about this trip *was* going to be a success.

The man onshore had turned his attention to the skipper. Maxie had the basics of Spanish, but she fell short where colloquialisms were concerned. 'Is he offering to help us?' she called out.

'Something like that,' the elderly skipper admitted sheepishly.

I bet, she thought, hoping Señor Acosta would have more charm. She stared at him again and quickly looked away. There was something in the man's eyes that said he had the sort of experience no woman with any sense would choose to get close to. And Maxie had plenty of sense. Though she was lousy at relationships, Maxie conceded with a shrug. Her ideal date was a civilised chat in a civilised restaurant with a civilised man—not a walk on the wild side with a barbarian with an earring and tattoos. She couldn't deny the man's edgy good looks had stirred something inside her, but he was food for her fantasies and nothing more.

'Are you from the bridal agency?' he demanded in a deep, husky voice.

'That's right,' she confirmed, halfway across the sloping plank. 'Could you give me a hand?' She had stopped in the middle of the plank, uncomfortably aware of the turbulent water churning greedily beneath her feet. If he'd grab her suitcase she could hold the guide ropes with both hands.

'Try walking tall,' he suggested. 'Look where you're going instead of looking down...'

Thanks very much. She'd take her chances with the fishes. But when he turned his irritation on the skipper she'd had enough. 'If you have anything to say, you can say it to me,' she insisted in Spanish. 'I chartered the boat, and I made the decision to sail to the island.'

His gaze darkened. 'You speak our language?'

'I would have recognised your tone of voice if you'd been speaking in Ket...a language spoken only in Central Siberia,' she muttered to herself—but he heard her.

'If you're so clever you should have more sense than to persuade an old man to bring you out to the island in a storm.'

Addressing his next words to Fernando, he spoke in a very different tone. 'You look chilled to the bone, Fernando. You will stay in the guesthouse until the wind drops. I'll have Maria come over with hot food and clean linen for you.'

'Si, Señor Acosta, y muchas gracias.'

Señor Acosta? Maxie groaned inwardly. 'So you're Diego Acosta?'

'Correct,' he confirmed.

The ironic twist to the firm mouth might make her senses roar but this wasn't the best of starts. Acosta might look more like a dangerous pirate than an international polo player, but his co-operation was crucial as he part-owned the island. 'I'm very pleased to meet you, Señor Acosta,' she said as she stepped with relief onto the shore.

Ignoring the hand she had extended in greeting, he turned away.

Diego Acosta wasn't sophisticated and he wasn't charming. He certainly wasn't her usual type of wedding contact, who looked to Maxie for guidance. The idea of this man looking to anyone for direction was a joke.

'Give me your bags, Fernando,' he called out in Spanish, staring out to the boat over her head.

Diplomacy was an essential part of her skill set, Maxie reminded herself. She had dealt with plenty of difficult characters in the past—starting her training on her father, who had been a Class One bully when she was younger, before illness had reduced him to a shell. She had learned how to handle him and she would learn how to manage Diego Acosta—though she would have to be subtle. She couldn't risk offending him. The Acosta family was so powerful they could destroy her hard-won reputation at a stroke. 'I'm Maxie Parrish,' she said, stepping in front of him so he couldn't ignore her. 'Holly's wedding planner?'

The dark gaze blackened. What the hell had she said now?

Parrish? Memories festered inside him, though common sense told him Parrish was not an unusual name.

'I spoke with Holly before I left the mainland—' the girl was explaining.

'Parrish?' he interrupted, powerless to stem the tide of memories.

'Yes, Maxie Parrish,' the girl repeated. 'From a company called Dream Weddings. Holly said she'd call to warn you I was arriving today.'

'She did,' he agreed, 'but she forgot to tell me your name.'

'Is there a problem with it?' she demanded, smiling faintly.

'Not at all,' he assured her in the same detached tone. 'I suppose I was expecting someone older.'

'I wouldn't send anyone else to scout a job,' she assured him in the same courteous tone. 'I always make the first visit and the last, Señor Acosta, as well as every other visit in between.'

She said this as if it were a gauntlet she was throwing down, but pleasantly. He wasn't fooled. He could sense the steel beneath the accommodating manner, and his hackles rose even as more basic needs surged in response to this intriguing combination of feminine fragility and rock-solid resolve. Either way, with his brother on a polo tour and his bride-to-be at his side, Diego was stuck with their wedding planner—like it or not.

Diego Acosta was staring at her and frowning as if he thought they might have met before, which was impossible. She never forgot a face—and would never forget a face like his. 'I can only apologise if this is a bad time for you—'

And then she saw the cane.

She should cut him some slack, Maxie resolved. A man like Diego Acosta, stripped of his full physical powers, would not be having a *bad* time—he would be having the worst time imaginable. She had researched the family to get a sense of who they were, and knew one of the brothers had been injured in a riding accident, but she hadn't realised he was still suffering or that he would be her host on the island.

'I'll take your suitcase,' he offered brusquely.

Disaster struck as he lifted it. His cane skidded on a

stone and he stumbled. She reached out to save him, but it was the worst thing she could have done. Cursing viciously, he snatched his arm away and made off in the direction of the car park with one leg dragging badly. In the faint hope of building bridges, she chased after him.

'I hope the weather's better than this in June,' she yelled against the wind. Even limping with a cane he had opened up quite a gap. 'This might not look like a great venue at first sight, but I'm not easily put off.' She wasn't even sure if he'd heard her. They were heading down a stony path in the direction of a car park, where the only vehicle was a powerful off-roader. 'Holly assures me the island is beautiful in June…'

He wheeled around so suddenly she almost cannoned into him. 'And what do *you* think, Ms Parrish?'

With Diego Acosta towering over her it was hard to think at all. 'I haven't seen enough to make a judgement yet,' she said honestly, wondering if her heart would slow down long enough for her to breathe. She had never experienced this sort of reaction to a man before, but Diego Acosta exuded a powerful sexual energy, which for someone with below average experience of men was quite something to take in.

'Do you expect me to show you around?' he asked, wincing as he eased his leg.

'How kind of you to offer,' she said mildly. She could feel the resentment crackling round him, but she wouldn't want anyone to see *her* in pain, either—and at least he wasn't bundling her back on the next boat. 'I look forward to hearing everything you can tell me about the island.'

'I can see this is going to be an interesting trip, Ms Parrish.'

Her composure was shattered by a single, burning glance. 'My thoughts exactly,' she agreed, wafting the hair out of her face with a suddenly shaking hand. 'Shall I put my suitcase in the back?'

Her intention had been to save him the risk of stumbling again, but she'd only managed to create more offence.

'I'll take it,' he snapped, his expression darkening as he swung her heavy bag from the ground as if it weighed nothing.

'That's very kind of you. And please don't worry, Señor Acosta. I won't be hanging around. This isn't a pleasure trip for me—it's purely business.'

'What else would it be?' Folding his arms, he leaned his tight hips against the side of the vehicle.

Her heart juddered uncontrollably. Diego Acosta might be the most arrogant man on the face of the earth, but her body liked him—far too much. 'All I need while I'm here is a map and a bike,' she explained, doubting any woman could remain immune to quite so much man.

'A bicycle? On these mountains?' Resting his stubble-blackened chin on one shoulder, Acosta shot an ironic glance at the jagged peaks surrounding them.

'A motorbike,' Maxie explained. 'Your brother, Ruiz, said you have one on the island?'

'Did he?' Diego Acosta replied coolly. Dark eyes narrowed in suspicion as he stared at her. 'I trust you're not suggesting I lend you my bike?'

Her stomach tightened as he straightened up to his full, imposing height. 'I ride a bike at home.' She had the satisfaction of seeing surprise colour his arrogant gaze, but in the interest of good business she decided not to push too hard on this yet. 'I quite understand if you'd rather not lend your bike to a stranger—'

'You haven't seen my bike,' he said, with all the confidence of a man who hadn't met too many women like Maxie before. 'I think you'd be safer taking the Jeep.'

She recoiled at the put-down, but all she said was thank you. Who liked being patronised? But this wasn't about Maxie's pride. She was here for the bride, and to earn the money that kept her father safe and well looked after in a nursing home. Glancing inside the vehicle, she hoped Diego Acosta would take the hint. He might be impervious to the elements, but she was freezing cold and wet. She was glad when he swung the door wide, and launched herself into the welcoming warmth of the luxurious interior.

'Now we wait for Fernando,' he announced, bringing the gale from hell with him as he entered the vehicle. Tossing his cane in the back, he swung into the driver's seat using just the formidable power in his arms.

She hoped they wouldn't have to wait long. Every part of her was prickling with awareness in the confined space. They were seated so close—too close. To distract herself she reached inside her bag to find her business card. 'You can check me out on this website.' She held it out to him. 'There are plenty of reviews from satisfied clients. I'm sure you won't be disappointed with the services I offer.'

'I should hope not.'

Something in Diego Acosta's voice made heat curl low in her belly in a way that was both inconvenient and inappropriate. Silence was her safest bet, Maxie concluded, noticing he barely glanced at her card before stowing it in a pocket on the door, where it would probably stay until it yellowed.

Fernando joined them soon after, much to her relief. She gripped the seat as they drove off, but she needn't have worried as Diego Acosta drove with the same arrant confidence with which he appeared to do everything else.

'How long do you plan to stay, Ms Parrish?'

'That's hard to say…' Her senses sharpened when he met her glance. 'Except I'll be as time-efficient as I can be.' She guessed this was to reassure them both. She had a real sense of invading the dark space of a man who had retreated to this remote island after his accident and who wanted to be alone—and she was in no hurry to stay a moment longer than she had to.

'How do you normally proceed?' he demanded.

'I spend a few days researching the bride's preferred venue, deciding if it's viable or not, and then I make suggestions, with photographs to illustrate my thinking.'

'And when the weather's like this?' he said abruptly, making a gesture that encompassed the storm ravaged landscape outside the windscreen. 'How do you tempt the bride then?'

'The sky seems to be brightening,' she pointed out, determined not to be put off at such an early stage. 'The bride is already in love with Isla del Fuego, Señor Acosta, and please believe me when I say I won't get in your way.'

'I can't see how we can avoid each other on such a small island.'

She tried reasoning that he'd been injured and craved solitude, and yet had been thrown into the path of a wedding—the most social of occasions. No wonder he was climbing the walls. But did he have to kick her on the way?

'You're very quiet,' he observed.

Staring at impossibly strong forearms and powerful yet sensitive hands could do that to a girl. She quickly dragged her gaze away.

'Are you regretting your decision to arrange a wedding here, Señorita Parrish?'

'On the contrary, my mind is buzzing with ideas.' He needn't know the details.

'Your name?' he queried thoughtfully as they slowed to take a bend. 'It seems familiar to me. Are you sure we haven't met before?'

'It's quite a common name.' She said this to a soundtrack of Fernando snoring. 'I'm sure we haven't met before. I would remember. And I doubt we move in the same circles.'

'What do you mean by that?' he said, frowning.

'Just that I have never been to a polo match and I doubt you crash weddings.'

'I'm surprised you haven't added polo to your list of things to do,' he said sharply. 'You have been hired to arrange the marriage of a high-profile polo player.'

His concerns on behalf of his brother were understandable. 'I've read a lot about the game, and I've watched a lot of films regarding the sport, documentaries—you know.'

'Which is hardly the same thing as attending a match.'

'That's something I intend to put right as soon as I can. I'm looking forward to it,' she added keenly. 'It looks such a thrilling game!'

'It is.'

She could have bitten off her tongue when he shifted position to ease his leg.

'How long have you been in the wedding business, Señorita Parrish?'

'Please—call me Maxie. Everyone does.'

'Are you going to answer the question?' he said, ignoring the olive branch.

'Both Holly and your brother have my references,' she said, rattled by this inquisition.

'It's a simple question.' Diego Acosta swung the wheel

so abruptly she was thrown into the side of the vehicle as the off-roader lurched onto a minor road. 'Why should I read your references when you're sitting next to me and can give me the answers yourself?' he added, with a certain amount of justification and a whole heap of ire.

Because she had edited her CV so carefully, maybe? 'I'm happy to answer any question you care to put to me.' Within reason, Maxie amended silently.

There was a lot of information about herself that she didn't share—like the fact she had been in business since the onset of her father's illness and the cost of his nursing care meant she couldn't earn enough working for anyone else on a fixed salary. She had struck out on her own, determined and desperate, with one goal in mind: her father's dignity and privacy had to be preserved. And it had been. And would continue to be, whatever provocation Diego Acosta tossed her way.

CHAPTER TWO

'I'VE been arranging weddings for friends for as long as I can remember.' Maxie had decided that if she was going to be forced to explain herself she might as well take the lead.

'And why would they ask *you?*' Diego Acosta demanded.

'I guess because I was always the one who put on events at school. Arranging weddings turned out to be a natural progression of that.' She only now realised that that was exactly what had happened.

'How long is it since you left school?'

'I'm twenty-six.' And enough was enough. 'I've been a successful wedding planner with my own company for over five years now, Señor Acosta.'

'My brother led me to believe that his wedding planner would be someone older with a great deal of experience. And excuse me for saying so,' he added, not sounding in the least bit sorry, 'but you seem far too young to handle a job of this size and importance.'

'All weddings are important to me,' Maxie said, bridling. 'And though I realise you are unlikely to have heard of me, please don't judge a book by its cover, Señor Acosta. I may not wear a business suit while I'm traveling, any more than you wear one when you're down on the dock, but I'm serious about what I do. And excuse *me* for saying so,' she added, thinking it better to get things straight from the off, 'I'm not your brother's wedding planner. I was hired to do this job by Holly Valiant.'

'I'm sure you'll agree with me that Holly has a some-what rose-tinted view of the island?'

'As I said earlier, I haven't had a chance to make any assessment yet. I'm completely impartial at the moment.'

And not about to roll over, Diego realised, fighting off the interest this provoked. If Maxie Parrish had anything to do with it this wedding would happen—and he was on notice. He couldn't remember the last time anyone had decided his agenda.

'I do wonder,' she said, distracting him, 'if the island falls short in so many ways, why you chose to come here to recuperate?'

'I beg your pardon?' He couldn't believe she had voiced those thoughts. No one mentioned his injury in front of him. No one even risked glancing at his leg. His brothers might—his sister Lucia definitely would. *But strangers?*

'Sorry if I'm being nosy,' she said. 'I'm just curious as to what drew you here.'

'Childhood memories,' he said sarcastically, hoping that would shut her up. Everyone had tiptoed round him since the accident. No woman had ever challenged him. Yet this kid had jumped right in!

'Whoa—slow down,' she said, grabbing his arm as he stamped down on the gas.

He glanced at the tiny hand on his arm. She looked too, and quickly withdrew it. 'I thought you liked speed?' he mocked her, in a pointed reminder of her claim to ride a motorbike at home.

'I ride my bike responsibly,' she said mildly.

She wasn't scared to take him on.

Seducing the wedding planner had never been part of his plan. It still wasn't. He must have too much time on his hands even to let thoughts like that occur to him. The type of woman he favoured was older and knew the score. She knew how to dress and what to say. More importantly, she knew when to remain quiet. She did not look like a fresh-faced tomboy, who dressed like a boy and insisted on speaking to him like a man.

'Are you all right, Fernando?' She had turned to check on the elderly skipper.

'My apologies if I woke you, Fernando,' he said, glancing in the rearview mirror.

The old man was more interested in hearing what Maxie had to say. *'Soy muy bien... Gracias,* Maxie,' he was saying, in a fonder tone than Diego had heard him use before.

When the girl had settled back in her seat she shot a glance at him. Was she reassuring him that Fernando was okay? Or was she playing it her way and to hell with him? She might look like a kid, but there was a lot going on behind that shrewd grey gaze, and he couldn't help wondering what other surprises Ms Parrish had in store for him.

'And when exactly did you learn to skipper a boat?'

'I helped to crew a yacht once—a friend at school. Her father was mad for sailing.'

He shot her a look that suggested *she* was mad. He couldn't believe she had thought it safe to transfer such tenuous experience to the open ocean in a barely seaworthy tub, but it told him something about her. She wasn't afraid of a challenge. Her cheeks pinked up when she caught his cold, assessing stare. Those pink cheeks told him everything he needed to know. Maxie Parrish might think she had all the answers, but she had none where he was concerned.

A client was always right. A client's brother-in-law-to-be had rights also—just so long as Diego Acosta didn't mistake her for a doormat. He had begun questioning her again about how she had grown the business so quickly. His lack of confidence in her was no big deal. It took time to win a client over. And, in his favour, the fact that this wedding was so important to him showed a strong family bond between Diego and his brother Ruiz.

'I had arranged quite a few weddings already when I was asked to plan one for a friend who works in television. She was so thrilled by the results that when she returned from honeymoon she asked if I could present a wedding feature for Valentine's Day—the perfect wedding, that sort of thing. Everything took off from there and I haven't looked back since.'

'But you haven't organised a wedding on a small island, where deliveries are uncertain and the electricity supply is erratic at best,' he pointed out.

'That's true. But generators can be hired, and I would have any supplies we need shipped over well in advance. I'm happy to take on the challenge.'

'I'm sure you are. And you're nothing if not prepared.' He shot a glance at her wet clothes.

'Had I known I would be sailing a boat today, I would have worn something more appropriate.'

'Why *were* you in charge of the boat?' He glanced at Fernando through the rearview mirror.

Maxie checked too, only to find Fernando was snoring again. 'Fernando was feeling a little unwell and I was glad to help out.' She left it there. Maybe Diego Acosta was trying to catch her out or embarrass her, but whatever his motive she wasn't going to land Fernando in trouble. 'I enjoyed the experience,' she said, brushing it off as if the terrifying voyage through raging seas had been nothing to her, 'and I never make the same mistake twice.'

'I should hope not,' Diego Acosta replied.

For some reason she was staring at his lips. She quickly looked away. She might be soaking wet and freezing, but her body was distinctly warm. 'If Holly decides to hold her wedding here and we encounter any problems, rest assured. I will deal with them.'

'That's what you're being paid for, isn't it?'

Diego Acosta grimaced and eased his leg as he spoke. She'd already worked out his mood was largely affected by pain or lack of it. 'It *is* what I'm being paid for,' she confirmed. And now she was wondering why, with all the money in the world to buy the best treatment available, the injury was still troubling him. And if it hurt so much why didn't he just take something for the pain, like everyone else?

'If this job is going to be too much for you, I'd rather you said so now,' he said, throwing her a lifeline she was supposed to grab eagerly and with gratitude, Maxie suspected.

'I always make a full evaluation before I come to any decision,' she explained calmly.

Her work as a wedding planner gave her such an intimate window into people's lives it wouldn't be the first time she had been invited in only for a client to draw back and ask themselves if this stranger would be sensitive to their needs, or if their most intimate secrets were about to be raked over and exposed to public scrutiny. Just because Diego Acosta was a testosterone-packed hunk it didn't mean she would treat him any differently from the rest.

'I think I've already explained that I won't need to trouble you for most of my time here.'

'*If* you stay on the island,' he said, as if this was by no means certain.

'Why wouldn't I?' she countered, careful to keep her tone bland and friendly. 'Judging by your earlier remarks, I assume you wouldn't want Fernando risking his fishing boat a second time in a storm.'

The elderly skipper chose that moment to stop snoring, and lost no time endorsing her words with heartfelt agreement. Maxie guessed Fernando was in no hurry to leave Isla del Fuego until he had received some coddling from Diego Acosta's staff.

'If there's a hotel here,' she added, 'I don't even need to trouble you for a room.'

'This is a small private island, with a small resident community,' Diego Acosta pointed out. 'There are no hotels, as such.'

'Perhaps bed and breakfast in a private house?' Maxie suggested hopefully.

'You will find no fairy godmothers on Isla del Fuego with rooms to spare, Señorita Parrish,' Acosta informed her.

No wonder. If there *had* been a fairy godmother her wand would have withered to a twig by now.

'You will stay with me,' he said, with zero enthusiasm.

Maxie's throat dried. Stay with him? Yes, it made sense, but—

When in doubt, smile and say thank you. That was the advice she always gave to anxious brides. 'Thank you,' she said politely, and as that seemed to be the end of Diego Acosta's welcome speech she directed her attention out of the window, to where the stubborn sea mist was lifting away like the curtains in a theatre, drawing back to reveal a scene that would make any audience gasp. Dramatic black peaks soared directly out of the raging sea, while at the side of the road luminous green foliage, made brilliant by the rain, competed for attention with striking banks of magenta blossom. 'How wonderful,' she murmured, forgetting the thunderstorm at her side for the moment.

'I wouldn't get your hopes up,' Diego Acosta commented, with a particularly male brand of humour. 'I live a rough, spare bachelor's life on the island, with very few home comforts.'

'I was referring to the view,' Maxi explained, chalking one up to the wedding planner. 'It's absolutely stunning.' And absolutely perfect for the wedding of a passionate couple like Holly and Ruiz, she thought.

Diego said nothing, but she noticed his fist tightening on the wheel. She guessed he would have preferred her to be a walk-over who would have given up on Isla del Fuego long before now, leaving him to brood alone. Hard luck, mister!

Did he read minds too? Maxie wondered when Diego Acosta shot her a glance. She was out of her depth here and they both knew it. She wasn't exactly a vestal virgin. She knew enough about sex to hope that one day she'd meet someone who knew what they were doing. Diego Acosta knew. She could feel it. While he, like the hunter he most assuredly was, must have felt her heat as she responded to him.

'There's just one thing,' he said.

Only one? 'Yes?' she enquired politely.

'While you're here you'd better call me Diego.'

She trialled the unfamiliar syllables beneath her breath. And shot bolt upright when she saw the look on his face. 'Diego it is,' she agreed, wondering if this might be just another ploy by Señor Acosta to make her feel uncomfortable.

'While you stay on the island there are conditions,' he said, adding to this suspicion.

She listened carefully as he listed the risks she might encounter on a volcanic island. She appreciated the heads-up, but it didn't change her mind. Diego Acosta was by far the biggest danger she was likely to encounter.

'Stray into caves and get lost—' his tone of voice brought her back to full attention '—or climb peaks that are unstable and I won't be able to help you.'

'Bottom line: it would be unwise for me to go adventuring on my own,' she said briskly.

'Correct,' he said. Relaxing back, he fell silent.

Maybe it was the hypnotic swish of the windscreen wipers, or maybe she had been too long out at sea, but the words just shot out of her mouth without the slightest intervention from her brain. 'Perhaps it would be safer if you showed me round?' she suggested.

'Me?' The black stare was incredulous.

She back-pedalled furiously, not wanting Diego Acosta to think she couldn't handle this on her own. 'Or I'm sure there's someone else who can show me round—Fernando, for instance?'

'Shouldn't we let Fernando enjoy his break?'

She could hardly argue with that.

'I'll take you,' Diego Acosta offered grudgingly.

Touring a mysterious island with Diego Acosta was not something a sensible woman would choose to do, but then he added, 'Who knows the island better than me?'

Maxie could only respond with, 'Thank you. I welcome any help you can give me. For Holly and your brother's sake, I think we should both do our utmost to make this visit a success.'

A cynical smile greeted this, though Diego Acosta's gaze remained fixed on the road. 'It appears my brother's fiancée has the most determined of champions.'

'She does,' Maxie confirmed, wondering if it would ever be possible to relax while Diego Acosta was around.

'Is something troubling you?' he prompted.

'No. Nothing.' She was staring at his thighs, Maxie realised, quickly looking away. They both looked equally impressive to her, but as that clearly wasn't the case she couldn't help wondering if he might benefit from the same massage therapy she had used to ease her mother's pain. 'I was just starting to plan,' she said, arranging her face in a thoughtful expression.

'Plans based on what?'

'Plans based on what I've seen so far.'

'They must be flimsy plans,' Diego observed, slowing the vehicle. 'Fernando,' he said, glancing in the mirror, 'this is where you'll be staying until the weather settles.'

'*Gracias,* Señor Acosta,' the old man enthused.

Maxie stared out of the window at a picturesque dwelling painted blinding white. Lovingly restored, it had a flower-festooned entrance and brilliant green shutters either side of tall, arched windows. A cactus garden framed the villa in vivid spikes of green, while the glittering black lava in which it was planted provided a dramatic contrast. Beyond the unusual garden the ocean was slowly turning from sullen grey to crystalline blue beneath a rapidly brightening sky.

'Do I get out here too?' She was keen to investigate further.

'No, you stay in the vehicle,' Diego ordered as he opened the door to get out. 'Unless you want to share the single bedroom with your skipper?'

'No, thank you.' Maxie firmed her lips. Each time she

thought she was getting the hang of dealing with Diego he had some new taunt up his sleeve. And that slack she had thought she should cut him? She was all out of rope.

Maxie sat in the vehicle, tapping her fingers on her bag as she watched the two men stroll up the path. They appeared perfectly happy to leave her to her own devices…

He might have known Maxie wouldn't stay where he'd left her. He had barely walked through the door when her heart-shaped face appeared at the window. Fernando beat a hasty retreat upstairs. He couldn't blame the old man. It was time someone informed Señorita Parrish that while she was on the island she did as she was told. He gave her a black look when she smiled at him—his body responded also.

'This is nice,' she said when she walked through the door, ignoring his hostile manner as she stared around. 'Do you mind?' she said, lifting her camera.

'You're here. You might as well.'

She was already snapping away, while he was trying not to acknowledge the pleasing scent of rain-washed air she had brought with her into the house.

'Perhaps some of the wedding guests could be housed here,' she mused out loud.

'I'll have to see if the cottage is available.'

'I'm sure you can make it so,' she countered, with a smile he guessed she used on all her clients. 'This place is beautiful,' she enthused. 'Did you design it?'

'What do you think?'

She cocked her head to look him straight in the eyes. 'I'm guessing no.'

'You'd be right.' He thumbed his stubble as he watched her at work, cursing the ruined leg that forced him to prop himself up against the wall.

'Everything's so well put together,' she observed as she clicked away.

'Blame my sister Lucia.'

'Oh, I think she's a marvellous designer.'

'I'll be sure to tell her you said so.' He vaguely remembered Lucia saying that her hard-nosed brothers must understand that mellow furnishings and comfortable sofas were essential if they didn't expect their guests to live like horses in a barn.

'I love this!' Maxie exclaimed, touching one of the hand-painted vases reverently.

He hummed and shrugged, refusing to admit that seeing what Lucia had done through Maxie's eyes was a surprise to him too. Her final camera shot was one of him. 'Holly will adore this,' she assured him confidently. Having checked the image first, she brought it over to show him.

Her scent, her warmth, her physical presence after he'd been so long alone almost overwhelmed him. 'Let's draw a line under this,' he said brusquely, barely glancing at the image. 'I have things to do.'

'Of course,' she said, putting her camera away. 'I'm sorry if I've delayed you, but I was just thinking we could use this room in some of the backgrounds for the album.'

'Really?' he said, wanting this over with. But in spite of his impatience his gaze found time to stray to her lips.

'Settings like these,' she was explaining, 'will give such personality and uniqueness to the photographs. And these stone walls are lovely,' she added, stroking them thoughtfully.

He was more interested in watching those small hands trace the centuries-old stone, until his leg chose to throb a warning that he wasn't match-fit—for polo or for women.

'I'm sorry,' she said, mistaking his grimace for a look

of disapproval. 'I must be keeping you.' Another few moments passed. 'Are you all right?' she asked.

'Yes,' he bit out, but his damaged leg called him a liar and dragged as he moved past her to the door. Anger erupted inside him. The fact that Maxie's breathing had speeded up when he brushed past her only heaped more humiliation on top of him.

'Don't worry—I'll shut the door for you,' she offered.

Catching hold of the door before she could reach it, he slammed it shut behind them, consoling himself with the thought that he had dealt with more wilful ponies than he could count, and the harder they were to handle at the start the better they pleased him when he finally broke them in.

He seethed all the way to the Jeep. Tossing his cane in the back, he swung in and Maxie jumped in beside him. Her lithe, agile form was another unintentional smack in the face for him, but as she turned to close her door her hair, which had dried into an inky cloud, brushed across his naked arm. He inhaled deeply, dragging in the scent of vanilla and lavender—a delicate and ultra-feminine combination he would never have expected the business-like Maxie Parrish to choose.

'Hurry up,' he blazed as she fumbled with her seat belt. 'I don't have all day.'

'You've really been very patient,' she agreed. 'I can't thank you enough for showing me the cottage, and I promise not to take up so much of your time in future.'

He hummed sceptically in reply. She was good at pretty apologies. It remained to be seen how she behaved when he piled on the pressure. It hadn't escaped him that the faster Maxie worked the sooner she would be out of here—and he could get back to licking his wounds in private.

CHAPTER THREE

HOLLY hadn't warned Maxie what to expect when she arrived at the Acosta family's holiday home, so when Diego drove over the brow of the hill she gasped. The elegant stone building looked more like a palace than someone's occasional home.

Reaching for her camera, she asked, 'Could you stop here for a moment?'

Diego Acosta drove on.

He had said he was in a hurry, Maxie remembered as the viewpoint disappeared behind them, and she could always come back alone.

She couldn't have been more surprised when he drew to a halt on the cliff edge and with a nod of the head indicated she should get out here. Not very gallant, but she'd take what she could get.

She had to concede he was right. This was a much better view, Maxie realised as she climbed down from the vehicle. The palatial old house sat on the top of a black lava cliff. At the foot of this a ruffled silver ocean stretched to the brightening horizon. The rain had stopped and the wind had dropped. She hoped the fresh air would clear her head, and made a play of fiddling with her lens to buy some time away from him.

'If you angle your camera like this...'

She started at the sound of Diego's voice. She hadn't even heard him coming. Lightning bolts shot down her spine when he reached across to tilt her camera.

'You can capture the house framed by the mountains on one side and the ocean on the other,' he explained. 'It's a famous view.'

Thankfully, he backed off while she worked, swiftly and efficiently, remembering he'd said he had other things to do.

'That was a great camera opportunity. Thanks for stopping,' she said when she joined him in the Jeep.

The massive shoulders eased in a *so what?* shrug. 'Research is what you're here for, isn't it?'

'That's right,' she agreed, putting her camera away neatly in spite of the fact that Diego Acosta's darkly glittering glamour was distracting to the point where her fingers were co-operating like sausages. She was used to men who came in uniformly drab design and were all the safer for it.

They drove into the Acosta holiday home compound through some impressive wrought-iron gates and turned into a cobbled courtyard framed by lushly planted flowerbeds. The planting was in stronger colours than Maxie was used to, but it worked here—the scale, the colour, everything was bold. In the centre of the courtyard there was a fountain, spurting plumes of water into the air, while shrubs and trees softened the edges of the old stone house. And the house, far from being the gloomy lair she had half expected Diego might inhabit, appeared to be a beautifully restored piece of history that had been loved and cherished over the years.

He parked at the foot of a wide sweep of stone steps at the top of which stood an older woman in front of some solid-looking double doors. The doors were open wide in welcome, and were flanked by twinkling windows that gave an impression as warm as the woman's smile.

'Welcome to Palacio Acosta,' Diego said. 'Or as some have dubbed it,' he added with a cynical curve of his lips, 'Palacio Too-antiquated-for-words.'

'Well, I think it's lovely!' Maxie exclaimed, wondering who on earth could have said such a thing. The thought that it might have been one of Diego's ex-girlfriends made the hair stand up on the back of her neck. Not that it was any of her business.

'May I introduce our wonderful housekeeper, Maria?' Diego said politely, standing back at the top of the steps so the two women could meet.

'I'm very pleased to meet you—' The words were barely out of Maxie's mouth when Maria gathered her close for a bear hug. If Maria worked for a monster she was certainly resilient, Maxie reflected when the house-keeper finally released her.

'I'm going to check the horses,' Diego said, swinging away. 'Maria will show you where everything is.'

'Thank you. And thank you for collecting me at the dock.' She hadn't expected him to stick around, but it would have been nice. *Nice?* It would have been chal-lenging, electrifying, and all the other words associated with extreme sport. 'See you later.'

Business came first, and bearing in mind Diego's warnings about the terrain she thought it wise to arrange an agenda with him so they could discuss safety issues further.

Turning, he gave her a look that made Maxie wonder if she had sounded desperate. 'I imagine our paths will cross again as we're living in the same house,' he ob-served coolly.

'Whenever suits you.' She didn't need to turn her back

to hide her red cheeks. He'd already gone. Unaccountably she felt the loss of him already, Maxie realised as Diego limped away.

The moment he was out of earshot, he rang his brother. 'What the hell are you trying to do to me, Ruiz?' Diego demanded furiously, grimacing as he leaned back against a fence post to ease the pressure on his leg.

'If I knew what you were talking about,' Ruiz replied, 'maybe I could help. Your temper certainly hasn't improved,' he observed. 'My advice to you is to get back on the polo circuit as fast as you can.'

'Don't you think I want to?' Diego roared over the crackling line to Argentina, where Ruiz was currently playing the game they both loved, with Holly cheering him on from the sidelines. Shouldn't Holly be here to deal with her pain-in-the-ass wedding planner? 'Don't you think I'm obsessed with getting back into the game?' he flashed on the heels of this thought.

'I've never heard you so angry before,' Ruiz commented laconically.

'We might be brothers, Ruiz, but there are limits to what I'm prepared to do for you. I came here to recover in private—not to play host to some confetti addict.' He stopped at the sound of a muffled protest, and then sighed as his soon to be sister-in-law, the well-named Holly Valiant, seized the phone from his recently re-formed playboy brother.

'You won't have to do a thing, Diego,' Holly promised him breathlessly from the other side of the world. 'Maxie is the most fantastic wedding planner. She will do everything. You *have* met her?' Holly prompted when he said nothing. 'She *has* arrived, hasn't she?' Holly asked with growing concern.

'She's here,' he confirmed flatly.

'Brilliant,' Holly enthused, completely missing the warning note in his voice. 'There's nowhere else on earth I would rather be married than Isla del Fuego.'

'You will have to excuse me, Holly,' he broke in politely. 'I have things to do. We can talk about your wedding some other time.'

'Oh...' All the air left her sails. 'Of course,' she said quickly. 'I imagine you're busy with the horses.'

Another long silence followed, and he could imagine Holly wondering if she'd said the wrong thing again. 'Yes, I'm busy with the horses,' he confirmed, to put her out of her misery. His attention switched to the ponies in the paddock, and to the one in particular that had fallen on top of him during the match. Months had passed since then, and the horse looked well and was moving easily—which was more than could be said for his owner, Diego reflected grimly.

'Is there something wrong?' Holly asked, forcing him to refocus on the call.

'Not really... There is one thing. The name of your wedding planner.'

'Maxie Parrish?' Holly supplied with her usual enthusiasm. 'She's great, isn't she?'

'Could you put my brother on the phone?' he said, keeping his voice carefully neutral.

'Of course...'

He could hear the strand of anxiety in Holly's tone, and then she covered the handset and said something to his brother.

'Diego?' Ruiz drawled, in a voice that suggested there were plenty of things he would rather be doing than talking to his brother.

'Parrish?' Diego drove on. 'Holly's wedding planner is called Maxie *Parrish*.'

'So?' Ruiz queried.

'Parrish,' he repeated.

'Dream Events is the name of the company, isn't it?' Ruiz remarked vaguely, clearly far more interested in his bride-to-be than anything else. 'Her references checked out. Even I was impressed. There must be thousands of girls with the surname Parrish, Diego. And, anyway, you should be over that.'

Maybe he should be, but he wasn't.

'It can't be the same family,' Ruiz said confidently.

'And you know this for a fact?'

But Holly had seized the phone again. 'Have I done something wrong?' she said. 'Please tell me if I've done something wrong, Diego.'

'You have done nothing wrong,' he soothed.

Where could he begin? And why rake up the past and ruin Holly's romantic moment? She wasn't to blame for a tragedy Diego had set in motion all those years ago.

'Would it be better if we rang you some other time?' Holly was asking with growing concern.

'No,' he said, making a conscious effort to gentle his tone. 'Tell me about the plans you'd like for your wedding, Holly.'

He felt bad when he realised all the fizz had left her voice, but she soon recovered, and as Holly started telling him her exciting news he drifted back to a black time in his life when he had taken one too many risks with tragic consequences. His time out now, with his injury from the polo field, could only be a relief for his opponents— for when Diego played he remembered what he'd done, and when he remembered he cared for nothing. Which made him a danger not only to himself but to everyone around him.

'You should get back to the game,' Holly told him softly, as if she could read some of these thoughts. 'You're needed, Diego. Your brothers need you. The team isn't the same without you.'

He hummed. 'I'm trying, Holly.'

'I know you're training every day. Things will get easier, Diego—trust me. And if it's my wedding that's bothering you—'

'There *are* other places you could get married,' he pointed out as Maxie's face flashed into his mind.

'But none as beautiful as Isla del Fuego,' Holly argued.

He gazed in silence across the paddock towards the sea, seeing the view as if through Maxie's camera lens. It was a scene of almost theatrical grandeur, he conceded. The pewter sea, in perfect accord with his mood, thundered against the black lava cliffs, casting diamond spray into the air. *And when the sun shone…*

'Are you still there, Diego?' his brother demanded, having taken the phone from Holly.

'I'm still here,' he confirmed. In body that was true, but his mind had strayed back to the past.

'How many people in the world have the surname Parrish?' his brother demanded. 'I know that's what's worrying you. Come on, Diego,' Ruiz insisted impatiently. 'You're the numbers guy in the family. You should know.'

This was true, and was thanks mainly to their elder brother Nacho, whose foresight and love had saved Diego from the blackest despair. Back in his arrogant youth Diego had lost money in a deal gone unimaginably bad, and it was Nacho who had told him that if Diego wanted to handle money he should learn how. Diego had gone

on to train as an accountant, and now controlled all the
family finances.

'Are you still there, Diego?' Ruiz pressed.

'I'm still here,' he confirmed.

'You're far too tense,' Ruiz commented dryly. 'And
I think we both know the reason for that. According to
Holly, Maxie Parrish is a good-looking woman, and you
are on the island together—practically alone. Have you
lost your edge, Diego?'

He stared down at the receiver as if this was news to
him, and then said, 'Maybe I'm not that interested?'

'And maybe you're kidding yourself!'

'And maybe you're in danger of sharing the same rose-
tinted spectacles as your bride.'

'Leave Holly out of this,' Ruiz warned.

'All I need is a sound leg, a good mount and a chance
to get back to the game I love,' he thundered.

'We'll talk again when you've come to your senses,'
Ruiz said, leaving him staring in frustration at the phone.

'What a wonderful home!' Maxie exclaimed, turning
full circle to soak up the atmosphere in the elegant and
welcoming hallway as Maria bustled round with pride.

'This house has been in the Acosta family for generations,' Maria explained.

'What a marvellous heritage,' Maxie said, thinking
back to her own, very different family home. The father
who had been so unkind to her mother when she was
young had been broken by her mother's illness. It had
been a struggle for him to keep up with all the extras her
mother had needed, so, understandably, home comforts
had been low on his list. When a hole had appeared in the
sofa Maxie had thrown a rug over it, and on one famous
occasion she had deconstructed a carpet sample book to

patch the stairs. 'My mother would have loved this,' she said wistfully, turning slowly to take everything in. She hardly realised she'd been speaking out loud until she felt Maria's compassionate touch on her arm.

'Come,' Maria insisted, shepherding her towards a magnificent mahogany staircase.

There was no patching here. An impeccable runner in mellow earth tones climbed the polished stairs and was held in place by gleaming brass stair rods. The effect was both impressive and cosy.

It was too late to help her mother now, or to wish that her parents' lives could have been easier, but at least her work allowed her to earn enough to make her father's last years comfortable.

'Please,' Maria encouraged, pointing to Maxie's camera.

The Acosta home was so much more than a sum of its parts, Maxie realised as she looked at everything through her lens. The rugs were a little faded, and had been worn thin by the passage of many feet, but they were all the more attractive for that. Everything was a little rough around the edges, she noticed now, but that only added to the ambience of a much-loved home. It was a warm, happy home, and she could feel the influence of previous generations all around her.

'I love this house!' she exclaimed impulsively. She loved the grand piano sitting discreetly beneath the sweeping staircase, with a stack of music to one side as if the pianist had just stepped out for a moment. She loved the family photographs clustered on top of it, and the scent of beeswax in the air. 'There couldn't be a better setting for a family wedding,' she said to Maria.

'*Perfecto,*' Maria agreed, nodding and smiling as if she and Maxie were as one.

'I'm going to call Holly right away and confirm her choice of venue,' Maxie enthused, remembering that first there was another call she had to make…

Her first evening with Diego loomed. Oh, good, Maxie thought wryly, wondering how that would turn out as she brushed her waist-length hair for the umpteenth time. Blue-black and gleaming now she'd washed the salt out of it, her hair lifted and floated around her shoulders in most un-Maxie-like abandon. She usually tied it back for business. She had intended to tie it back tonight, but for some reason she wanted Diego to see her looking relaxed, for him to know that he didn't scare her.

Though goodness knows what they'd talk about, Maxie mused as she studied her perplexed reflection in the mirror. What she knew about polo could be safely inscribed on the top of a pin, while Diego was hardly the typical wedding cake fanatic. But this was work, and she'd get on with it. Replacing the silver-backed hairbrush on top of the lovingly polished French antique dressing table, she stood and frowned, remembering the news from the nursing home hadn't been good. Every day she hoped for improvement, knowing deep down it would never come.

She must remain focused on her work, Maxie reflected, firming her jaw. Work kept her grounded. Work paid the bills. Work kept her father safe.

Walking across the faded Aubusson rug to the beautiful old armoire, she picked out one of her 'all occasions' dresses. In pale cream silk it was equally suitable for an up-town business meeting or supper with friends. It was the dress she chose when she didn't want to look as if she was trying too hard. She teamed it with a pair of discreet nude-coloured sandals, then applied some shadow to her eyes, and some lipgloss. Now she was ready to face the tiger in his lair.

It was hard to remain tense in such a beautiful setting, Maxie realised as she walked across the room. Mellow evening light was streaming through the French doors dressed with filmy white muslin, while the open windows brought the scent of the beautifully tended gardens into the room. The bedroom was incredibly feminine, with several flower arrangements she had no doubt Maria had arranged, while a grand old four-poster bed took centre stage. Draped with floating ivory fabric, it had a beautiful hand-stitched quilt that picked up all the various pastel shades. She would never choose to decorate a room so prettily herself, but she loved it so much it made her wonder if she'd grown up practical because she'd had to be, or if practical was her nature. The only certainty was that tonight she was having supper with an unpredictable man, Maxie concluded. And he was probably counting down the seconds until she left.

'Diego!' It took her a moment to gather herself when she found him standing outside her room. 'Are you waiting for me?'

He was leaning against the wall, and the look he gave her suggested Maxie was in serious danger of flattering herself. 'I was on my way down to supper,' he said, giving her a lazy once-over. 'I presume that's where you're heading too?'

She was burning from his scrutiny while *he* looked amazing. How was it that some people only had to throw on a pair of jeans and any old top to look good? She could smell the soap from his shower, and his thick black hair was still a little damp and curling wildly round his swarthy face, catching on his stubble. But when he straightened up and she saw the cane propped against the wall

she knew he had probably stopped outside her room because his leg was hurting him, and as they walked towards the head of the stairs she tried to measure her
step to his without making it seem too obvious. His leg
seemed stiffer than ever tonight, and she wondered if the
damp weather had affected it. Hanging back, she could
see how heavily he was relying on his cane.

He was glad Maxie was behind him and couldn't see
the surprise on his face. Discovering the young tomboy
transformed into a poised and confident woman had been
a revelation to him. But why was he surprised? She was a
successful businesswoman. He just hadn't had it thrust in
his face before. She looked stunning in the simple dress,
and he could imagine her walking into a meeting and
getting any terms she wanted out of her suppliers—an
image that irritated him when he thought of the men she
would meet in the course of her work. Perhaps Ruiz was
right about the route to rehabilitation and relaxation.

Right on cue the muscles in his leg stabbed a warning that he was more likely to grind his jaw in pain than
soften his lips to seduce Maxie.

'I love your house,' she commented as they walked
downstairs.

'It isn't strictly mine,' he said, putting her straight.
'The family shares it.'

'Don't you think that's why it's so lovely?' she
said, pausing to examine an old oil painting of some
disreputable-looking ancestor.

The Acosta men hadn't changed that much, he reflected, then, realising Maxie was waiting for him, wondered if she was taking it slowly on purpose—making
allowances for him?

'I think it's a real family home,' she said, oblivious to
his blackening mood.

'Yes, it is,' he said, waiting for her to go first before he tackled the last flight of stairs.

'Don't you love this hallway?' she said, trailing her slender fingers down the mahogany banister as she reached the hall ahead of him.

He concentrated on her naked shoulders and the cascade of silky black hair tumbling in luxuriant waves to her waist. This led him on the shortest of journeys to the neat curve of her buttocks, clearly visible beneath the clinging fabric of her dress.

'Well, I think it's perfect!' she said, turning to look at him.

'I can't see much wrong with it,' he agreed.

'How wonderful to have holidayed here when you were children. I love visiting houses like this.'

The last girl he had brought to the *palacio* had asked for the 'powder room' in order to touch up her make-up. Then she'd told him she hated the house. It was so dated, she said, proceeding to give him a list of requirements for her next visit. Fortunately the sea had been calm that day. He'd shipped her out on the next boat.

Maria was in the kitchen with an array of dishes that would have fed an army of gourmands. He ate in silence, while Maxie and Maria chatted away like old friends. Maxie handed him an agenda of things she wanted to cover, and he might have been surprised by her approach if he hadn't seen her dressed for business as she was tonight. He accepted the paper from her, glanced at it, and got on with his meal, wondering again about the tomboy who could transform herself so convincingly into a sophisticated businesswoman in no time flat. Did she have a boyfriend—a lover? Maybe she had children? He didn't know anything about her. Maybe she was married? That thought made him tense.

When they had finished the meal and the dishes were being cleared away—a duty Maxie had insisted on sharing with Maria—she tossed him a cloth. 'Wipe the table down, will you?' she asked him casually. 'While I load the dishwasher?'

He stared at the cloth in his hands while Maria, clearly in shock, bustled across the room to take it from him. His grip on the cloth tightened. 'Take the rest of the evening off,' he told Maria. 'You deserve it. And thank you for a delicious supper.'

'*Gracias, Señor...*' Maria said, backing out of the kitchen as if she never wanted to forget the sight of him holding a cleaning cloth.

Maxie had her back turned to him as she continued clearing up. When she'd switched the dishwasher on, she straightened up and turned round. 'Would you like to see the shots I've taken so far?'

Remembering the quicker Maxie got what she'd come for, the quicker he could be alone again, he said, 'Why not?'

He had to admit Maxie surprised him yet again. She might be an excellent wedding planner, but her photographs were also out of the ordinary. She had shown the island in a way he'd never seen it before, highlighting aspects which transformed it from a forbidding prison into a treasure trove of possibilities. Seeing Isla del Fuego through Maxie's eyes was a revelation to him.

'Is something wrong?' she asked when he grimaced.

'No. Everything's good.' Except his leg, which was cramping again. 'Your photographs are very good.'

'Thank you.' She turned to go. 'An early night for me, I think,' she advised him as she headed for the door.

Animal instincts battled with his common sense, while his leg screamed in protest. *'Buenas noches, señorita,'* he ground out as she left the room.

CHAPTER FOUR

SHE had had the worst night's sleep ever. Was it wrong to want a man who looked like a pirate to behave like one? Was it crazy to lie in bed wondering what would happen if she crept to the door and left it temptingly ajar? As if she'd be so stupid. She wouldn't have the first idea of what to do if she *had* done something so ridiculous and Diego had walked in. She had heard him coming upstairs and remained absolutely still as she'd listened to the water run while he took his shower. She had imagined him standing beneath the spray naked. No wonder she'd had a sleepless night.

Leaping out of bed, she drew the curtains on a brand-new day. The sun was shining and it was hard to believe she had been greeted yesterday by stormy skies and a glowering man. Opening the window and leaning out, she dragged in the scent of blossom and grass, intensified by the refreshing rain and now the warmth of the sun. So where was Diego? She glanced round the empty gardens, guessing he'd be with his horses. She'd take a shower, make her calls, and then she'd check the agenda she'd given him. She had no time to waste on fantasies involving dangerous men sweeping sensible girls off their feet and carrying them away to make passionate love to them until they couldn't stand.

But she was only human, and Diego Acosta was one heck of a man.

He had been up before dawn, after a restless night spent tossing and turning at the thought of a woman he wanted in his bed sleeping in a room just down the landing.

So what had held him back?

Slamming his cane against the wall with a vicious curse, he took a shower and changed into clean jeans, desert boots and the first top that came to hand. Opening his bedroom door, he found her walking down the landing towards the stairs.

'Good morning, Diego,' she called to him, oblivious to his black mood. 'I hope you slept well?'

'Maxie,' he said briefly.

'Are you coming down to breakfast?' she asked as she ran down the stairs.

Was he supposed to follow at a snail's pace?

'Maria has promised to make pancakes today,' she called back to him as she hurried across the hall towards the kitchen.

She looked so fresh-faced and innocent in her simple top, blue jeans and sneakers. 'I'm going to check on the horses,' he said, craving fresh air and the empty pampas.

'No problems, I hope?' she asked, pausing with her hand on the kitchen door.

Problems? What? More than she could see as he moved stiff-legged down the stairs? 'One of the ponies kicked my best horse last night,' he ground out.

'Oh, no!' she exclaimed with concern. 'I'm so sorry. No lasting harm done, I hope?'

'I don't know yet,' he snapped, frowning. Socialising was good for recovering horses, but there was always the risk they might get hurt, and he felt responsible for what had happened. It was another black mark on the day.

'Perhaps I can see your horses later?' she suggested.

Before he had a chance to refuse this request she had disappeared inside the kitchen. His black mood thickened when he heard her laughing with Maria. She was really making herself at home.

Thanking Diego's housekeeper for the delicious breakfast, Maxie reflected on the many amusing tales Maria had told her about Diego growing up. It was probably just as well he hadn't joined them in the kitchen, or Maria almost certainly wouldn't have opened up the way she had. Maxie had been her usual guarded self. She never talked about her childhood, and preferred to look to the future and build rather than waste time thinking about what couldn't be changed. She had spent too many nights barricaded in a room with her mother when her father had returned home drunk after yet another failed business deal to want to look back. Her own relationships with men had scarcely fared any better. She seemed to have the knack of finding younger versions of her father. No wonder creating events for other people suited her so well. She had long preferred to view the world from a safe distance.

She was scarcely back in her bedroom when her father called her on her mobile. 'What a great surprise,' she said, her face wreathed in smiles.

'Don't ring me now,' he howled. 'It isn't convenient!'

'But you called me,' Maxie pointed out, all her elation evaporating.

'Can't you remember the simplest thing, Maxine?' her

father bellowed, as if she hadn't spoken. 'I have a board meeting at nine. I've got no time for your jabbering now!'

'Dad, I'm sorry—' But the line had already been disconnected. He was as confused as ever, she realised. Her father hadn't attended a board meeting in his life, as far as Maxie knew, and he wasn't about to start now.

She took a moment to compose herself, and then sniffed and straightened up. Checking her reflection in the mirror before she left the room, she remembered her father's nursing staff telling her to get on with her life. They were probably right, but it had been so long since she had pleased herself, without making her responsibilities top of the list, she had almost forgotten how.

Or maybe not, Maxie thought. A faint smile touched her lips when she spotted something interesting in the courtyard. It wouldn't hurt to take a closer look.

Diego had checked the horse and was satisfied the wound was superficial. Having returned to his room to take a shower, he was rubbing his hair dry when the messaging service on his phone trilled. It was a text from an anxious Holly, wanting to know what he thought of Maxie. Were his feelings supposed to have changed towards Maxie since Holly's last call?

He texted back: *She's here. She's fine. Doing her job, as far as I can tell.*

Holly texted back immediately: *Is that it?*

That's it, he confirmed, stowing the phone. What else should there be?

He was just easing his leg when he heard something that made him lurch across the room as fast as he could to stare out of the window. With a violent curse he left his bedroom in such a rush he forgot his cane. With his stiff leg lagging behind, he used the brute strength of his upper body to swing down the stairs, and, limping across the seemingly endless stretch of hallway, he launched himself at the front door and flung it wide. 'What the hell do you think you're doing?'

'Oh, hello,' Maxie replied, turning on the seat of his prized custom-built Harley. 'I hope you don't mind. I saw your bike and I couldn't resist!'

She looked pretty hot on his bike...

And she was making no move to dismount.

She caressed the controls.

'I hope you weren't thinking of taking my bike for a ride?' he derided, making what, without his cane, was embarrassingly slow progress down the steps.

'I have ridden a bike before.'

'Not like this, you haven't,' he fired back at her, cursing beneath his breath as he closed the distance between them at a limp.

'I'm not a child, Diego...'

That much he could see for himself. And there wasn't so much as a trace of guilt in her eyes. 'Do you normally take things that don't belong to you?'

'I wasn't taking it. I was sitting on it,' she protested.

A flashback to his past fuelled his anger. He had first started riding bikes with a friend who was dead now. That thought led to the name Parrish banging in his head. 'Don't you dare,' he warned as Maxie's fingertips strayed dangerously close to the controls.

She had never done anything like this before. She had never rebelled or taken anything that didn't belong to her without asking permission first. She had been all business, all correctness and restraint for so long she couldn't imagine what she was doing.

'Off,' Diego commanded, in the coldest voice she had ever heard.

She could accept she was doing something wrong, but was it that bad? Something inside her flipped. 'Okay, so you don't want this wedding here. I get that. You don't want me here. I get that too. But as your brother part-owns this island, and his fiancée has hired me to give an opinion, I'm going to stay until I'm in a position to do that.'

'Then get back to work and get the hell off my bike!'

'I've done my work,' Maxie raged back. Springing off the bike, she took a stand. 'For your information, I stayed up half the night to finish my work. Holly will have my report the second she wakes up. What have *you* done apart from feel sorry for yourself?'

Diego paled. 'What did you say?'

'Isn't that what this is about?' Maxie demanded as all the pent-up feelings she had suppressed for years burst out of her. 'So you can't play top-class polo? You can still ride a horse, can't you? You're still breathing!'

'I should stop there, if I were you,' Diego warned her quietly.

'Why? Does the truth hurt, Diego? How long have you been on the island, exactly? Are you *never* going home? And if the pain's so bad why don't you take painkillers like everyone else?'

'You're really pushing it, lady…'

'Am I?' she said, standing her ground when he took a step towards her. 'Perhaps it's time someone did. Maybe I shouldn't have sat on your bike—but for God's sake, Diego, it's only a bike. I was hardly going to roar away on it. Where would I go?' she demanded angrily, staring around. 'This was an island the last time I looked!'

'Are you finished?' he demanded, looking more fero-cious than she'd ever seen him with his ruggedly beautiful head thrown back, earring glinting, black eyes blazing.

Absolutely, devastatingly, gorgeous...

As they glared at each other Maxie slowly began to realise that the attraction between them was mutual. She drew a sharp breath in as Diego came towards her. Incredulity mixed with excitement and sheer blind terror at what she had stirred up churned inside her. He backed her towards the bike. She could feel the cool metal against her overheated skin and the leather seat pressing into her back. Passion boiled in Diego's stare—in hers too, she had no doubt.

'Next time ask me first,' he ground out.

She gasped as he seized her arm. 'Get off me!'

What was more terrifying? The cold, blind fury in Diego's eyes, or the cruel twist of his smile? Just his grip on her arm was alarming. But as they stared it out it was as if they were joined in some deeper, primal way. Almost as if they were meant to be like this—close, passionate, exclusive and intense.

'I said, get off me!' she raged.

Diego merely angled his chin to stare down at her, as if she were a particularly interesting wild creature of a type he had never encountered before.

'Don't you hear me?' She tried and failed to shake herself free. 'Don't you dare look at me like that—don't you dare smile!'

Diego's answer was simple. She dragged in a shocked breath as he swung her off her feet and dumped her back on the saddle. Swinging in front of her before she had chance to protest, he started the engine and kicked the stand away. 'You want a ride?' he snarled over his shoulder. 'Then I suggest you hold on.'

A red mist clouded his vision as he powered up the

bike. Maxie hadn't just breached his privacy, she had opened Pandora's Box on the past. She had insulted him. She had—

No. He refused to contemplate, even for one second, that she might have held up a mirror to his face. He wanted her, but he also wanted her gone. He couldn't inflict himself on anyone—his leg, his mood, the danger that lurked inside him, all of it poison. She wanted to know why he was here on the island? For everyone's safety. That was why. She had chosen to ignore the warnings. Her bad luck. She hadn't seen him like this. She hadn't seen him with the devil on his back.

They shot away so fast she almost fell off the bike. She clung to Diego as he accelerated, taking the bike at such speed round the first corner that his jean-clad leg brushed the road. Yes, she had ridden a bike before—it was the easiest way to cut through the London traffic—but there was a world of difference between her 125cc commuter bike and Diego's white-hot Harley.

At first all she could think of was not falling off, but gradually she realised that Diego could ride a bike at speed as well as it could possibly be ridden. She still clung to him like a limpet. Forget prudent, sensible behaviour—this was a matter of staying alive. Resting her cheek against his hard, warm back, she felt his muscles flexing, and against all that was sensible she felt safe. The grey top he was wearing held the scent of soap and warm, clean man. And at least she didn't have to look into those mocking eyes, Maxie consoled herself—though she did have to be careful where she put hands that badly wanted to explore Diego's muscle-banded torso. Of course she wouldn't let them—any more than she would acknowledge the effect of sustained vibration on a body that had been too long without sex.

When he finally stopped the bike she dismounted shakily.

'Well?' he demanded.

'Awesome!' she exclaimed, before realising Diego expected her to be broken by the experience. But it had been amazing. And if he didn't like it… 'I can't believe I waited so long to do that,' she said, finger-combing the tangles out of her hair. 'You're an amazing rider.'

Easing onto one hip, he stared at her long and hard. 'You must be a sucker for speed.'

'Maybe I am,' she agreed.

Ruffling his hair, he turned away. He couldn't pretend she hadn't surprised him. Maxie Parrish was fearless. Was he in such a hurry to get rid of her now? Maybe having company wasn't all bad. At least Maxie had something about her. Behind that cool exterior was a leather-clad biker-girl with a ferocious temper—which made him wonder what other passions lurked beneath the surface of Maxie's carefully manufactured veneer. He'd have to be unconscious not to want to find out.

Did they actually have something in common? Maxie wondered, exhilarated by the bike ride. Had the same jolt of electricity joined them briefly?

'What now?' she pressed, feeling she could cope with anything. Her lips pressed down with disappointment as she gazed around at the uninspiring shrub and rock. Nothing could compete with that bike ride, and this was the dullest part of the island she'd seen so far.

He only now realised that the passion driving him had brought them to a very interesting part of the island. 'The Green Caves,' he informed Maxie.

'I don't see anything,' she said, staring around an apparently empty stretch of ground.

'That's because you're not looking in the right place.'

He took in her flushed face and windswept hair. She looked great.

'Where am I supposed to be looking?' she said. 'There's nothing but scrub here.' She gestured around. 'This definitely wasn't on my agenda.'

'Neither was my bike,' he reminded her. 'Do you always play by the rules, Maxie?'

'It's the safest way,' she said with a shrug, but she didn't hold his gaze.

She followed Diego out of curiosity. She wasn't sure if this was a joke or not. There was nothing to look at of any interest—apart from Diego. He was still limping, but not too badly today. She guessed that was due to the adrenalin coursing through his veins after the ride.

'Welcome to the Green Caves,' he said, stopping dead in his tracks.

She followed his stare down to some stone steps cut into the ground.

'As we're here,' he said with matching cool, 'I might as well show you the underground caves so you can share the info with Holly.'

'Thanks,' she said briefly, relieved Diego had got used to the idea of his brother's wedding being held on the island.

'Once we're underground in the Green Caves you must stay close to me.'

No hardship so far. 'Okay,' she agreed.

'Did you put sightseeing on your list for the guests?'

'Yes,' she confirmed, ignoring his offer of a steadying hand.

'Hey!' he exclaimed, saving her from falling when she stumbled on the steps. 'I'm supposed to be the one who's compromised here.'

There was no humour in his voice, or on Diego's face

as he set her back on her feet, but it was the first time he
had mentioned his injury, and as steps forward went that
wasn't a bad one. 'Thanks,' she said casually as they carried on down the steps in what was almost comfortable
silence.

The staircase ended in an underground passageway,
dimly lit by some low-voltage lighting. 'We're under the
sea,' Diego explained when she paused to listen.

'And the lights?'

'Solar panels. Quite a recent addition.'

As he moved on she wondered if Diego felt more relaxed too. More importantly, she wondered if he registered her as a woman at all, or if she was merely someone
he felt he had to show round for the sake of his brother?
He had never looked more the pirate, with his harsh,
chiselled face, but that firm, sensual mouth belonged
to a more sophisticated sensualist altogether. And now
erotic possibilities were flooding her mind—which was
hardly helpful when she needed to be concentrating.

'The excavation of these caves goes back centuries,'
Diego was explaining. 'And as each new generation takes
ownership more improvements are made.'

'That sounds impressive,' she agreed, and her gaze
followed Diego's strong, tanned hand as it moved lightly
over the stone wall.

'I like to think so,' he said, shooting a keen glance at
her.

'After you,' she said lightly. There wasn't enough space
in the tunnel to pass him without touching.

He moved away.

They now entered a cavern the size of an aircraft han-
gar. Stalactites hung like weathered spears above their
heads, while dripping stalagmites lined the path. She
spotted a sheer drop on one side of the cave, but when

she went to take a closer look Diego held her back. He was by far the bigger danger, she thought, glancing at his hand on her arm.

'How deep is this chasm?' she asked him on a dry throat.

'Shall we find out?' he suggested.

Reaching into the back pocket of his jeans, he pulled out a coin. As it spun and flashed in front of her she wondered what it would be like to have Diego on-side, to have someone special to confide in, but then the coin landed in glassy water just inches from her feet and the illusion shattered into numberless ripples.

'The surface is so clear and still it acts like a mirror,' Diego explained.

Creating a false impression as misleading as her own far-fetched hopes and dreams, Maxie thought wryly. But it was a great place to bring wedding guests, and she told him so. 'Though I won't tell anyone about the coin toss,' she explained. 'I think we should keep that a secret between us so it has maximum impact for the guests when they discover the secret of the caves.'

'Do you like keeping secrets, Maxie?'

She balked at that. 'Sometimes,' she admitted. The caves suddenly felt oppressive. 'Is that it?' she prompted.

'There's just one more thing I think you should see.'

Her gaze lingered on his back as Diego led the way. He was such a powerful man, with only the limp to remind her that all was not well with him. If the leg had been attached to anyone else it might have been a good time to suggest trying out the massage technique that had worked so well for her mother—but not while it was attached to Diego Acosta.

The next cave contained an underground lake. A natural chimney allowed light to flood in, giving the water an unearthly glow. Diego was hunkered down at the water's edge, where tiny albino crabs were scuttling in the shallows at his feet.

'They are unique and vulnerable,' he explained.

Diego's hard face had softened. This was a side of him she hadn't seen before. It made her even more certain that she wasn't the only one who had allowed the past to colour her life. As she stared at the broad sweep of his shoulders and his strong, tanned neck she wanted to ask so many questions, but she was here for a fact-finding trip of the island, not him, and so she settled for, 'I didn't take you for a nature-lover.'

'Oh, I love nature,' he said, standing up to fix her with an assessing stare. 'It's people I have a problem with.'

Okay. She turned her attention to gathering more shots for Holly.

They held concerts in the underground theatre here, Diego explained as he led the way into the incredible facility buried deep in the bowels of the earth. 'We invite people over from neighbouring islands.'

As you do, Maxie thought wryly. 'How many people can the theatre seat?' She had immediately reverted back to business mode and was taking notes.

'Three hundred or so—more if we take the seats out.'

'It would be perfect for a party after the wedding breakfast,' she mused out loud, though of course it would be up to Holly to make the final decision.

She was standing too close to Diego, Maxie realised as her body thrilled a warning. Moving away, she stared down the steeply raked aisle to the unusual stone stage, with its backdrop of rough-hewn rock glowing amber beneath the lights. She took some shots, made a few more notes, and then turned to go—almost colliding with him.

As she skirted past she could hear his steady breathing above the thundering of her heart and something made her ask impulsively, 'Do you mind if I stop by to watch you training your horses?'

'You'd find it boring, surely?'

'No. But if I'd be in the way—'

'You wouldn't be in the way.'

If her heart had been thundering before, it was out of control now. 'Are you sure?'

'I'm sure.'

They climbed back up the steps and emerged into the light. 'Do you still think you can ride my bike?' Diego asked.

She stared at the big black monster, sensing there was a bigger decision to be made here than whether she could ride his bike. 'Yes, I do,' she said.

Diego needed someone to stand up to him. She needed to test herself. Bring it on.

CHAPTER FIVE

THE bike seemed to have grown bigger, while Maxie seemed to have shrunk. Drawing in a steadying breath, she tried not to register anything when Diego swung onto the saddle behind her—and failed miserably. Her back lit up like the Fourth of July. At least he couldn't know how she was feeling—and at least he couldn't see the tension on her face.

'Just thumb the starter button, Maxie.'

There was another moment when he reached around her to guide her hands and his hard, muscular torso pressed into her back. The temptation just to close her eyes and lean against him…

'Did you get that, Maxie?'

Diego's tone was enough to eject her from that daydream. 'Got it,' she confirmed.

'Good. You may have ridden a bike before, but I promise you you never rode a bike like *this* before.'

'Like everything else on the island, I'm sure it's extraordinary,' she said dryly, smiling as she turned on the engine. It purred like a kitten.

'Squeeze, don't grab at the controls,' Diego warned as she upped the revs. 'You have to make love to them.'

'I will,' she said briskly, not wanting to think about making love in any context right now.

'If you do exactly as I tell you,' Diego added, 'you'll find the bike will respond like a—'

Like a lover? 'Like a bike?' she suggested.

'Like the most responsive of bikes,' Diego amended coolly.

Blowing out one last steadying breath, she released the brake and hit the throttle.

'You're doing ninety,' Diego yelled above the wind. 'Slow down or I'm taking over!'

She laughed as exhilaration took her over, and only slowed at the next bend. She took the corner well and didn't speed up again. She'd had her moment. She wasn't trying to provoke Diego. She just wanted to push the boundaries for once in her life.

That was Maxie Parrish, Maxie concluded wryly as the countryside turned from a dun-coloured blur into a crystal-clear image of scrubland punctuated by the occasional tree, she always knew when to pull back.

'You ride well,' Diego commented now he could be heard over the engine.

She could only blame the island for freeing something crazy inside sensible Maxie. 'Thanks for letting me ride!' she yelled back.

As Diego eased back in the saddle, she felt the loss of him instantly.

'Do you ride a bike every day?' he said.

'Every day to work—and sometimes when I'm at home.'

'Home?' Diego queried, frightening her with the speed of his pick-up. 'Do you live alone?'

'I do now,' she said lightly.

'No boyfriend.'

'No…' She drew the word out as if she had no time for one, which was true.

'You don't live with your parents, then?'

'No.' She took a moment. 'My mother's dead.'

'I'm sorry for your loss,' Diego said, leaning forward to speak in her ear. 'My parents too—both of them.'

'I'm sorry.'

'It's been quite some time now.'

'But it never gets any easier, does it? I think about my mother every day. I still miss her. I always will. I suppose you just learn coping strategies.'

'I suppose you do,' Diego agreed, and then after a moment he added, 'What about your father, Maxie?'

Every part of her was instantly on red alert. 'He's retired,' she said, reverting to the one-liner that always got her through. 'He lives quietly now.' She waited tensely, and was relieved when Diego let the subject drop.

'Take a left here,' he instructed. They were almost back at the *palacio,* and were entering a fenced lane beyond which lay endless paddocks where countless horses were grazing.

She stopped the bike and Diego got off. With the immense power of his upper body he barely used his legs as he vaulted lightly over a gate. A sleek bay pony, instantly recognising its master, came trotting over. Nuzzling Diego's pockets imperiously, it consented to consume a packet of mints.

'Are you going to ride him?' Maxie asked almost simultaneously with Diego springing lightly onto the horse's back. His injury counted for nothing now. Nudging the horse into a relaxed canter, he was at one with it immediately—but she guessed that when it came to playing polo at a professional level the stiffness in Diego's leg would hold him back. Climbing the fence to watch, she rested her chin on her arm.

'I come here every day to train,' he explained as he cantered past.

She could understand why. The steady rattle of hooves was so soothing.

At least it was until another horse, wanting to join in the fun, bucked its way across Diego's path, causing his horse to shy and then to rear. Diego only just managed to stay on, and the effort wrenched his leg. Dismounting, he bent double in pain. Maxie felt sick and wished she hadn't been there to see it.

The one thing she knew she mustn't do was turn away and have him think she was disappointed in him. 'Can I help?' she called out when he didn't move.

He didn't look up as he waved her away, but she saw the grimace of pain on his face. She couldn't imagine what it must be like to have been at the top of his game only to stare failure in the face now, day after relentless day.

The first thing he did when the pain had passed was to check his horse, and then with a kind word he slapped its rump to urge him back into the field. When he limped towards her she said nothing. There was no need for words. Their eyes met briefly and that was it. In some ways it was the closest they'd come.

The hot red sun was sinking slowly behind the mountains as Diego rode the bike home. They had been out for hours and she'd hardly noticed time passing. The black peaks were framed in a shimmering gold, and even the sea had calmed into a smooth lilac disc. It was an incredible sight, but the day had gone flat. Diego took the bike at a modest speed, as if he didn't want to invite any more disasters. When they reached the house and she dismounted, he rode away without another word.

This feeling, like a lump of lead in her stomach, was

due to her getting too involved, Maxie concluded as she walked across the silent hallway. Did she really think she could ease Diego's pain? What if she tried and it didn't work?

What if, what if, what if...?

She was a doer, not a dreamer—wasn't she? How could she make things right for Diego?

Back in his bedroom, Diego raked his hair impatiently and swore as if that could blank out what had happened. What had possessed him to ride a horse in front of Maxie? Why had he let her watch? Why had he questioned her about her father and simply let it go? Was he afraid to hear the truth? Was he afraid to face the truth about his leg—his future—his place in the Band of Brothers polo team? Was he afraid to face the truth about Maxie?

The chances of one Parrish being connected to another in a world of individuals with the surname Parrish was practically non-existent. And if he asked her and there *was* a connection he doubted she would answer him honestly anyway. She would just strengthen her defences, making the elusive Peter Parrish even harder to find. It would save a lot of grief if he just hired a private investigator and waited until he had some answers.

He gazed out of the window at the pool house. There was still a very good chance he could make a full recovery. He had to believe that one day full feeling would return to his leg. One thing was sure—the enemy of his progress was inactivity. He'd take a shower and have a swim. If he could do nothing more than religiously practise the exercises he'd been given in the hospital then that was what he'd do.

* * *

Back in her room, Maxie picked up the phone to call Holly with the good news about the caves. 'Yes, I'm fine,' she confirmed when Holly spoke without breath or break about her concerns for Maxie. 'This isn't about me,' Maxie reminded Holly good-humouredly when she could finally get a word in. 'It's your wedding—though the next time you might warn me what to expect on the unreconstructed man front!'

'There won't be a next time,' Holly said, laughing down the phone. 'And I doubt anyone could warn you about the Acosta brothers. They're unique!'

'They certainly are,' Maxie agreed, laughing too. She went on to explain what she had seen and how she thought they could use the caves as part of the entertainment for the guests. They chatted some more and Holly thanked her for the photographs.

Maxie had crossed to the window by this time, only to see Diego crossing the garden. On his way to bed down the horses, she presumed. She pulled back just in time as he looked up, making her heart thunder and her body yearn.

This was madness, Maxie told herself firmly, finding she had to wait until even his shadow had disappeared before she could concentrate enough to finish what she'd been saying to Holly.

'Are you still there?' Holly demanded.

'I'm still here,' Maxie confirmed. 'I was just distracted for a moment.'

'By Diego?'

'How did you know?' she said, smiling.

'Maxie, please. Relationships are my business, remember? Agony aunt?' Holly prompted. 'My whole job revolves around sniffing out sparks.'

'There are no sparks.'

'Right,' Holly agreed without conviction. 'So, what do you really think of him?'

'I don't know what you mean. I'm here to arrange your wedding. I hadn't even noticed Diego, to be honest…'

'Oh, he *has* made an impression on you,' Holly interrupted with amusement. 'Remember, I have seen him—so nothing you can say will ever persuade me that you haven't *noticed* Diego. Did you even say that, by the way?'

'Could we concentrate on business and your wedding plans, please?'

'For now,' Holly agreed. 'So what do you think of the island so far?'

'Fabulous. Perfect for your wedding,' Maxie said honestly. She gave Holly some more back-up information to flesh out what she'd already told her. 'So if you're sure you're happy to leave everything to me—'

'That's why I hired you.'

'I'll send some more notes through later today.'

'Put some juicy bits in this time,' Holly insisted with a laugh.

'Not a chance,' Maxie exclaimed, pressing her back against the cool of the wall in the hope that it might soothe her overheated body. 'Sorry to disappoint, but this is strictly business, Holly.'

'Now you've upset me,' Holly protested, forcing a sob into her voice. 'I was planning on us being sisters-in-law one day, so I'll always have someone around to organise my life.'

'Well, as that's never going to happen—'

'All right—so concentrate on my wedding for now. Just think of it as a rehearsal for your own.'

'Holly,' Maxie warned in a mock-stern tone. 'Seriously.

Stop this.' And that was as far as she got before Holly laughed again and cut the line.

Did Holly even know Diego? Did she think for one moment he would look at someone like Maxie? Diego had been right about Holly—she did look at the world through rose-tinted spectacles. Getting to know Diego any better than Maxie already had would be the most insanely dangerous thing she could do.

And what if she wanted to?

She just had to get a hold of herself, Maxie told her inner voice impatiently, wishing she didn't feel quite so mixed up. After all the excitement on the bike what she needed was to cool down, Maxie concluded, searching for her swimming costume. She couldn't do any more work on Holly's wedding plans today so she might as well take some time to chill out—if that was possible while she and Diego lived under the same roof.

Grabbing her things, she was just about to leave the room when she decided to make a quick call first. 'Dad?'

'Maxie? Is that you?'

The fact that her father seemed to be totally switched on now, despite his earlier confusion, was incredible. 'How do you feel?' she asked eagerly, thrilling at the sound of his voice.

'Wonderful,' he assured her.

'That's the best news I've heard all day. And don't you worry. I'll be back before you know it to take you out, and we'll have a great time—'

'Take me out? Take me out where? Who is this?' her father quavered in a voice that chilled her. 'Why do you want to take me out?' he demanded suspiciously. 'What have I done? You can't blame *me*,' he exclaimed on a rising note.

And then he started yelling and swearing just like the

old days, only almost worse, Maxie realised, because now he didn't know what he was saying. She knew she should be relieved when a nurse took over the phone, but instead she just felt beaten. It took a good few steadying breaths this time before she could accept that it was her father's illness that had beaten them both.

'Everything's fine this end,' the nurse assured her. 'Are you okay?'

'I'm fine,' Maxie confirmed. *Fine. Fine. Fine. She was fine.*

Emotion filled the room, leaving no air to breathe. Ending the call, she gave herself a moment, waiting for the tide of emotion to pull back, as it did every time, only to regain its strength for the next onslaught. Drawing in a shaking breath, she checked she had everything she would need at the pool house. The thought of a brief spell of solitude and mindless exercise had never seemed more appealing.

Swimming was one thing Diego could still do really well. After years of training he had plenty of muscle power in his upper body, and if one leg worked less smoothly than the other the water supported it and he could still maintain a credible speed. And swimming was one of the very best exercises for his injury, the physios had told him. The cool of the water after the heated bike ride was certainly welcome. His regular stroke allowed him to focus his mind and plan his next move. With Maxie around the name Parrish was constantly in front of him, so it made sense to him to get to the bottom of the Peter Parrish mystery once and for all.

All he wanted was the chance to confront the man with what he'd done—what they'd both done. He hoped then he could start looking forward—maybe one day he might even forgive himself. Performing a powerful tumble turn using just one leg, he cruised to the side just as Maxie walked through the door. He huffed a humourless laugh, guessing she'd take one look at his scars and probably faint. Even his brothers had flinched when they had first seen them. Like the painkillers he refused to take, nothing could change the past, but to have her see him stumbling and scarred felt like some sort of penance. His guilt for what had happened all those years ago required constant feeding.

'Hello, Diego,' she said, seeming surprised to see him. 'You don't mind if I take a swim, do you?'

'Do you want to wait until I get out?'

'I can, if that's what you'd prefer?'

'No problem for me—help yourself.' He swung out of the pool on his arms and then, predictably, after his ease of movement in the water where he was weightless, he stumbled. It took him a moment to regain his balance and straighten up. As the pool water streamed from him he waited for the inevitable gasp.

'Is your leg troubling you again?' she asked, staring at it intently. 'I expect the adrenalin from the bike ride has worn off.' She laughed. 'Or maybe you've overdone it in the pool,' she said with more concern, glancing at the settling water.

Brushing past her, he reached for a towel. He saw her wince when he staggered, and the next moment she had reached out to grab it for him. 'I can pick up a towel without your help, thank you.'

'Oh, for goodness' sake, Diego!' Picking the towel up, she threw it at him.

Catching the towel knocked him off balance again, and he had to hop a couple of times before he could regain it. 'Well?' he demanded when she stood staring at him.

She could see that Diego was trying to keep the pressure off his injured leg, but what else had rattled his cage? The scars, Maxie guessed. They were bad. And she could imagine he didn't want anyone seeing them. Well, it was too late now. She could see a lot of scar tissue she was sure would loosen if treated with the proper emollients, which suggested to her that Diego had performed his exercises regularly to build back muscle power, but that he had neglected to treat the recovering skin.

And she wasn't here to offer a diagnosis, Maxie reminded herself firmly. She was here to swim. It was important to remain detached and businesslike, she thought to herself as she removed her sarong. *So that was why her hands were trembling.*

Thankfully her swimming costume was respectable in the extreme. She went swimming to exercise, not to flaunt her body, though Diego's lazy appraisal made her wonder why she'd bothered putting a costume on at all.

'This is a fabulous pool,' she said, giving herself an excuse to turn away. 'Would the wedding guests be allowed to use it?'

'Of course they would.'

Hearing the same tension in his voice, she decided to have it out with him. 'Have I done something to upset you? I apologise if I have. Or is it your scars?' she asked bluntly, unable to ignore the elephant in the room any longer. 'Do you think I can't bear to look at them? Do you think I'm revolted by them? Is that how shallow you think I am?'

'I have no thoughts on the subject at all.'

'Really?' she said in a challenging tone. 'Then please stop staring at me like that. If you don't want me to use the pool, I'll go.'

A cynical smile tugged at Diego's lips. 'Brave talk, Maxie.'

'Brave?' she said. 'You'd know all about that, wouldn't you, Diego?'

'What do you mean by that?' He wasn't smiling now.

'You're brave,' she said bluntly, holding his cold gaze without blinking. 'Everyone knows how brave you are. Don't you prove it each day you exercise to get your strength back? When we all know how monotonous that must be for you, especially with so little to show for it, and just the hope that some time in the future you'll be fully mobile again. Wasn't it a brave decision to let your horse live when everyone said his leg was beyond repair and he should be shot? Holly tells me a lot of things about you,' she said before he could get a word in. 'So if you're so brave you won't mind me touching your scars. You won't mind me massaging them—easing them—helping you...'

When he threw his fierce dark head back and laughed in her face, she added, 'Or are you just too damn proud to accept anyone's help, Diego?'

'You've got some nerve,' he grated.

'Yes, I have,' she agreed in the same calm voice, 'so you can stop with the menacing act. I'm here. I'm alone. And I'm not afraid of you. What are you afraid of, Diego? Failure? Are you afraid you'll never play top-class polo again? If that's the case you'll let me try to help you. If that's not the case, then you're just the most unpleasant man I've ever met!'

Diego was staring at her as if he couldn't believe what she'd said. But someone had to say it. She knew how hideous it must be for him to have her see him in pain, but she was here and there was no avoiding it. Better to tell him what she was thinking, rather than hide behind awkward politeness for the rest of her stay.

'I believe I can help you,' she said with conviction. 'I learned some massage techniques from a physio in the hospital and they helped my mother.'

'And do you really think I'm going to let you try them out on me?'

'Why not?' She held the hostile stare unflinching. 'What do you have to lose, Diego?'

'So where my physios have failed you think you can help me?'

'I can try,' she said quietly.

'One of these days you're going to meet yourself coming back,' he exclaimed with an angry gesture.

She could see where Diego was coming from. Yes, she was pushy, and, yes, she was taking a risk in offering to try, but she had always tried to help and she couldn't shake that off just because Diego hated her seeing him like this.

Everyone felt vulnerable sometimes. 'Please let me try, Diego. It can't do any harm, can it?'

His expression suggested she had better not get this wrong.

CHAPTER SIX

MAXIE was already regretting her reckless offer—maybe because her natural impulse to help had never been challenged by such rampant maleness before. Diego was relaxing on one arrogant hip and staring down at her, as if daring her to touch him—and the truth was she wasn't so sure she dared.

'There's oil on the table,' he said, with the mocking smile firmly fixed on his lips.

'What is this?' She turned the bottle in her hands.

It was a potion he had bartered for with some quack in return for a lead rope and a packet of mints. 'I don't know. It's massage oil. Does it matter what it is?'

As she turned to look at him he wondered if this was the moment when she'd make some last-minute excuse and pull out. But, no—removing the cork, she sniffed the liquid inside the bottle.

'It certainly smells like muscle relaxant.' Upending the bottle, she rubbed some between her thumb and fingers. 'And I think there are emollients in here too. I don't think it matters where it comes from, just so long as it works…' Her grey gaze held his steadily.

'Then you'd better get started,' he said.

She was right. He had nothing to lose. Let Maxie try her hocus-pocus on his leg. The risk of embarrassment to him was hugely outweighed by the thought of her dark head bent over him as she worked diligently with those tiny hands in an attempt to ease his pain—an attempt that would fail, but still…

'Well?' he prompted. 'It's time for you to put your technique to the test.'

Putting a towel on the lounger, to protect it, she indicated that he must stretch out on top of it. 'I'm going to warm the oil first,' she explained.

He had to admit that after so long a drought the sight of Maxie warming massage oil in her tiny hands was a provocation too far. Grabbing a towel, he covered himself with it. 'Do your worst,' he said, and then he closed his eyes to blot out the sight of both Maxie and his scarred leg.

What madness had brought her to this point? Maxie wondered as her oiled hands hovered above Diego's spectacular form. Telling Diego to relax was a joke when she was the one most in need of stress relief. The thought of touching him as intimately and as firmly as she must was a daunting prospect. But exciting too.

'I'm ready,' he prompted.

'Good.' And now she must ignore him and concentrate on what she had to do. She had helped her mother, but could she help Diego? *She had to help him.* Tugging a cushion off one of the other loungers, she put it on the floor at his side and knelt down.

'The injury is here,' Diego said, pointing to a place just below his knee. 'But it seems to affect all my leg right up to—'

She cut him off. 'I'll find it.' Closing her eyes, she inhaled deeply and began to work.

'Don't you need to see what you're doing?'

'Please be quiet.' She said this calmly, then explained

in the same soothing tone, 'If I close my eyes and concentrate it allows my senses to come into play. If you talk, I'm distracted.'

She heard him shift position restlessly. Diego didn't like to be told what to do. She was certain no one had ever told him to be quiet, other than perhaps his siblings, but as he relaxed and the stillness of the room enveloped them both she began to feel the resistance of damaged flesh and muscle beneath her fingers and worked with more confidence.

He couldn't believe he was allowing Maxie to do this. Struggling to relax, he knew that if she proved even one iota less than good he would shrug her off and never forget this intrusion into his private world. Dissatisfaction at being so slow to heal was steadily eating away at him without this interference from her.

'I'm not hurting you, am I?' she asked him as he flinched with self-loathing.

'No,' he snapped as she hit a tender spot.

Maxie's small hands were surprisingly strong, but then he remembered the heavy ropes she'd tossed to shore. She might be small, but in determination Maxie was not to be underestimated. Against the odds, he began to relax. He stared down at her dark, silky head as she worked. There was something about her touch, her scent, her calming approach, her very presence when he had spent so much time alone, that made her intriguingly different—and incredibly, beneath her skilful fingers, he felt his damaged muscles begin to yield and loosen. Having lived with pain since the accident, his relief was indescribable. Closing his eyes, he rested back against the cushioned headrest…

'Does that feel better?'

He couldn't believe he'd been asleep, or that her voice had wakened him.

'Well?' she prompted. 'Has it helped?'

He flexed his leg and could hardly believe there was just a low, throbbing ache where so recently there had been acute, stabbing pain. And the dull throb was probably due to the force of Maxie's fingers. 'It's a lot better,' he admitted.

'Well, don't look so surprised. If you patronise me I won't do it again.'

His mouth tugged in the first real smile. 'I shall consider myself chastened, Señorita Parrish.'

'You do that,' she advised. 'I'm going to wash my hands now.'

He caught hold of her wrist as she moved away and had the satisfaction of hearing her suck in a sharp breath. She stood trembling and aware as he held her, reminding him of one of his wild ponies. When they were first captured and brought to him they averted their gaze just as she was doing now, as if to look at him would be an admission that they wanted to stay. He felt how vulnerable she was beneath his huge fist, and how delicate her bones were. He could feel her pulse fluttering beneath the skin and felt some primal urge to protect her. For Maxie's sake he let her go.

She felt light-headed as she walked the length of the swimming pool on her way to the changing rooms. And that wasn't just the Diego effect—which was disturbing enough in itself. Her mother had always said Maxie had healing hands, and though Maxie had laughed at this suggestion sessions did take a lot out of her. She could only describe it as her own strength pouring into someone else. How did Diego feel about it? Why had he caught hold of her wrist? He had let her go again, she remembered wryly.

She took her time washing her hands. Closing her

eyes, she prepared herself for a return to a world with Diego Acosta in it and a wedding planner with an increasingly bad habit of straying from her brief. But at least she'd had good news to give Holly. Palacio Acosta had the best facilities for a wedding that Maxie had ever seen.

By the time she returned to the side of the pool Diego was standing on his good leg, flexing the other. 'Does your leg still feel better?' she said, hoping there hadn't been some unexpected reversal.

The dark gaze reached deep inside her. 'There is some improvement,' Diego admitted. A faint, attractive smile played around his lips, making a crease in his cheek. 'Same time tomorrow?' he suggested, pulling on his jeans.

She quickly averted her gaze and stared over his head. 'I'll see if I can fit you in,' she said.

'You do that.' Diego's dark eyes were amused as he fastened his belt. 'Or we could run a barter system,' he suggested, tugging a polo shirt over his head. 'I teach you to ride. You work on my leg?'

'Why not?' she said, still dwelling on his naked torso, covered now—unfortunately. 'That sounds fair.' And totally insane.

'I'd better find you a good ride,' he said, with the attractive crease back in his cheek.

'You better had,' she agreed.

And there it would have ended, with a good bargain made, had she not been trying so hard not to look at Diego when she walked past him. If she had been paying any attention to where she was going instead of avoiding his glance she wouldn't have tripped over the leg of the lounger and he wouldn't have been forced to catch her.

'Careful.' His face was only a breath away.

'Thank you,' she said, pulling away as if he had burned her.

'My pleasure,' Diego murmured, with a great deal too much insight in his voice and in his eyes for Maxie's liking.

This was like trying to take on the forces of nature single-handed, she concluded. Her heart was pounding a tattoo, and if she couldn't trust herself to behave what hope was there? But instead of taking things further as Diego so easily could have done, he let go of her arm and stood back to let her pass.

He wanted her. His hunting instinct was in full flood, but his instinct also told him to keep her safe. From him. He wanted to thank her for bringing him relief from pain, but he knew where that would lead. And he could sense that Maxie was vulnerable. In business she had all the confidence you would expect, together with the skills necessary to succeed, but in her personal life… He knew nothing about her personal life, except that she was innocence personified compared to him. What was she hiding? he wondered as he stared into her cool grey eyes.

Damn it. She hated being on the back foot. Diego had almost certainly guessed how much she had wanted him to kiss her.

'Are you coming?' he said, holding the door.

To buy time, she grabbed a couple of towels and waved them at him. She needed a moment. But she couldn't keep him waiting all day… 'Excuse me,' she said politely when she reached the door. The open space with Diego in it was far too small to pass without brushing against him.

'Excuse *me*,' he replied, but instead of moving away he moved in.

Catching her close, he smiled into her eyes, and with such exquisite confidence she could only gasp as he brushed her lips with his. And then he proceeded to tease her mercilessly with kisses to her neck, before pulling back as if to study the effect. He must have known she was lost. Closing her eyes, she pressed her palms flat against Diego's chest. Two could play at this game. She slowly traced the map of muscle to his neck and then linked her hands behind his head. Opening her eyes she found him smiling down at her.

'Maxie,' he murmured in a faintly chastening tone.

'Yes?' she whispered.

Taking hold of her hands, he gently drew them down again.

'Don't tease me,' she warned, ready to push all her past failures aside in the hope of achieving one perfect moment.

'Is that a challenge?' Diego asked, drawing her attention to his lips.

A dam burst inside her. Pressing against him, she reached up. Locking her hands behind his neck she exclaimed with relief when Diego's grip tightened. Dipping his head, he brushed her lips with his. Parting them with his tongue, he searched deep. It was a fiery exchange, as if she filled some empty part of him. He certainly fulfilled every one of her wishes. A wild sound escaped her throat when his hands first touched her breasts, and she shivered with desire when he caressed them with a tenderness that amazed her. He chafed her erect nipples until she could hardly breathe and every part of her was on fire for him. Her lips were bruised and swollen from his kisses—she loved his taste, his warm, clean-man scent. The urge to battle Diego's strength and share his passion consumed her, and uttering his name in a half-sob of desperation she thrust her hips greedily against the brutal thrust of his erection.

'Maxie—' It took her a good few moments to re-alise that everything had changed and that Diego was gently disentangling himself. She was lost in a world of sensation until he held her at arm's length to whisper, 'Enough...'

What had she done wrong? Why had he kissed her in the first place? Why respond to her at all if only to draw back now? And then, in the most humiliating and pro-vocative of gestures, he reached out to stroke her hair, as if he could tame her like one of his ponies, or pacify her like a child. 'Don't,' she warned, pulling back.

'Don't you think I know?' he said, holding her firmly in front of him. 'Don't you think I can read you like a book?'

'What do you know?' she asked, outraged.

'You can't use me to practise on.'

'Of all the arrogant—'

'You haven't enjoyed sex in the past,' Diego said, ig-noring her, 'and you want to know what it would be like. So what am I supposed to do about it? Throw you to the ground and ravish you? Is that really what you want?'

She had to wait until her breathing steadied before she could trust herself to speak. By then she was ready to accept that Diego had only responded to the signals she'd sent him and that she couldn't blame him for that any more than she could blame herself for wanting him.

She had to calm down and pull this back. How else could she continue working with Diego to make Holly's wedding day the best it could be?

'I'll see you at the house.' Diego said this in an im-pressively normal voice and he stood well clear of the doorway.

'Sure.' She knew she should be relieved he could turn it off so easily and knew she must do the same. 'I expect

I'll see you at supper,' she managed in her usual businesslike voice, as if she *hadn't* just flung herself at him. 'You go ahead. I'll gather up the rest of the things here.' Along with her senses, she hoped.

Diego walked off in the direction of the stables while Maxie clung to the fact that he had seemed to take their encounter very much in his stride. Not so good was discovering she was the type of woman he found so easy to resist. She couldn't pretend that didn't hurt—especially when every part of her had just woken up to the most amazing possibilities.

Diego was seething with anger, all directed at himself. He had ignored every one of his self-imposed warnings and paid for that with the discovery that just being close to Maxie was enough to rock his self-control. He was in the barn now, walking down the line of stalls, searching for the soothing effect the horses always had on him. Today it eluded him. He and Maxie lived different lives. Making love to her would be the easiest thing in the world, but a brief period of elation would be followed by regret. And what form would that regret take for Maxie? Hadn't he done enough damage in his life? For him, regret would only involve more self-loathing, knowing he had taken something pure and good, just because he could, and trashed it. He was bad news and Maxie deserved better. The animal inside him might be clamouring to be fed, but the man he was said no.

Maxie spent the next week working as hard as she could on Holly's behalf. She worked pretty hard at avoiding Diego too. When she had to meet up with him to work on his leg she made sure it was always under Maria's watchful eye. Diego wanted her to continue the treatment, and Maxie had to prove to herself that she could. What had

happened in the pool house couldn't be allowed to inter-
fere with his treatment when they could both see signs
of improvement.

Maxie had decided that the answer in the long term
was to train Maria, and ask Maria to pass on the knowledge to whoever could help Diego at his next port of call.

One evening, when she arrived in the kitchen, she
found him pacing up and down impatiently. 'You're here
at last,' he said, throwing her one of his black looks.

'Yes, sir,' she murmured dryly.

'I want you to come outside,' he said.

She looked at Maria for clues, but Maria just smiled at
her and shrugged, as if to say Maxie would have to wait
and see. The first thing she noticed when she stepped
outside was the huge bonfire. 'What are you burning?'

'Can't you guess?' Diego demanded as he matched
his stride to hers.

'Your cane!' One of the stable lads was stoking the fire
with it. But as she tried to grab it Diego stopped her.
'*Gracias,* Maxie,' he said, staring into her eyes.

She went blank for a moment, seeing nothing but him,
and then Maria was hugging her and the groom was
laughing as he fed the fire with more branches. 'You don't
need your cane!' she exclaimed as the penny dropped.

'I knew you'd catch on eventually.' Diego's eyes were
dark and amused.

'But what a massive turning point. This is wonderful!'

'You have no idea,' he agreed, turning serious.

'I do have some,' Maxie argued quietly.

'But I still get my treatment,' Diego threw back at her
as he turned for the house.

'So what about my riding lessons?' she called after
him.

Diego stopped dead in his tracks. That was a very nice

back view, she thought, wondering if Maxie Parrish and danger were joined at the hip these days.

'We start tomorrow,' he said, slowly turning to face her.

'Suits me,' she agreed, playing it as cool as he had.

Diego's recovery was all she cared about, but with that embarrassing encounter at the pool house still fresh in her mind she was going to have a word with Maria. Linking arms with the housekeeper, she outlined her plan.

'I'm ready for my treatment,' Diego announced, the moment Maxie walked through the door.

He was sprawled back on the chair where he usually sat when she massaged his leg, with his powerful arms stretched across the back of it as he regarded her through half-closed eyes. The slight smile on his face only proved how right she was to make some changes.

'There's been a change of plan,' she announced.

'Oh?' Diego demanded, instantly suspicious.

'*Sí, Señor!*' Maria exclaimed enthusiastically, bounding forward. 'Today I am to perform your massage!'

'What?' Diego's eyes were points of steel, but Maria quickly came between them and lost no time getting to work.

'I won't always be with you,' Maxie explained, as Maria pummelled and rubbed with all the fierce efficiency of a champion bread-maker. 'And I'm sure you'll agree that in Maria I couldn't have a better deputy. She'll pass on everything I've taught her to the next person, and so on...'

Diego's gritted teeth suggested Maxie would pay for this.

CHAPTER SEVEN

'So, you're frightened of me?' Diego observed—a little smugly, Maxie thought—when Maria had left them.

'Rubbish,' Maxie protested, concentrating on loading the dishwasher. She had offered to clear up, knowing how busy Maria was. She had taken up enough of the good-hearted housekeeper's time already.

'You can't trust yourself to touch me,' Diego mocked as he reclined in his chair.

'You wish,' she murmured under her breath.

'Why else would you deputise Maria?' Diego challenged.

'You're going to trip over that ego of yours one day,' Maxie observed coolly, stretching up on tiptoe to put some bowls on the top shelf. 'The only reason I asked Maria to help is so you won't be left stranded when I leave.'

'When are you planning to leave?'

Diego's sharp tone surprised her. 'My work here is almost done,' she pointed out, turning to face him. 'All the suppliers I need are in place for the wedding, and I've got a full programme of events planned. I'm only waiting for Holly's go-ahead.'

'Great,' Diego said, without enthusiasm.

Springing out of the chair, he stalked to the window

to stare out. She couldn't leave. There was too much unfinished business between them. He wanted to know more about Maxie—who she was, and why she was so reticent about talking about her family. He wanted to unearth Peter Parrish, and there was always that faint chance that Maxie might be able to lead Diego to him. Either way, he wasn't ready to let her go.

'Good,' he said, changing his plans as he swung round. 'It's time for me to go too. I've been here long enough, and thanks to you my leg is almost better. I'm match-fit and my horse has recovered. What point is there in staying?' He shrugged, a little pleased to see the surprise in Maxie's eyes.

She had put her challenge out there, hoping, she supposed, that Diego would talk her out of it, only to learn that he wasn't going to. So this extraordinary adventure was over.

Moving things round at the sink so he couldn't see the disappointment on her face, she resigned herself to a life of fantasy. She had seized life briefly, but then had taken fright and let it go again. 'It will be good to get back,' she said brightly.

'You're a terrible liar, Maxie.'

'I always tell the truth,' she argued as Diego's lips tugged in a smile.

'Do you?' he said.

'Yes,' she said hotly.

'I like that,' he commented, angling his stubble-blackened chin to stare at her.

'What?' she said, still churning inside.

'I like the way you've changed since you first arrived on the island. I like the way the buttoned-up business-woman has lost her bit and bridle on the island.'

Yes, but *he* didn't want to take advantage of it. 'It's

just a shame you haven't changed from the charmer who met me on the dock,' she countered.

'I think we've both changed,' Diego argued thoughtfully. 'But don't change the subject, Maxie. We're talking about you—not me. I want to know more about you.'

'Like what?' she said defensively.

'I'd like to know why you shrink back into that same defensive shell every time you take a call from England.'

'I don't!'

'Don't you?'

She exclaimed with shock when Diego dragged her close. 'So who is the real Maxie Parrish?' he demanded. 'Is it the buttoned-up businesswoman with the weight of the world on her shoulders? Or is it the firebrand who tore up the road on my bike?'

She tried to fight him as he kissed her, savagely and without break. Balling up her fists, she thrust them against his chest, only to encounter solid rock, but Diego broke away as quickly as he had claimed her.

'When are you going to be honest with yourself, Maxie?'

She was still shaking, her hand across her mouth as if that could hide the proof her arousal. How could she have allowed this to happen again? She stared at Diego with furious eyes, wanting to throw a punch at his arrogant mouth. She wanted to spit in his black, piratical eyes. She was panting and furious and—and inconveniently aroused, Maxie admitted silently as she fought for control. And while the urge to pummel the living daylights out of Diego was certainly one option, he had lit something inside her that refused to be extinguished.

Grabbing hold of him, she yanked him close and took what she wanted, and as much as *she* wanted, for as long as she wanted, until with a fierce, angry sound she let him go.

'*Dios!*' Diego murmured, wiping his mouth with the back of his hand as he stared at her in amazement. 'I knew I was right—but not that right!'

'Don't flatter yourself,' she flashed.

Turning abruptly, she left the room.

What now? Maxie asked herself, furious at her loss of self-control as she stalked across the courtyard on her way to who knew where. By the time she reached the fence surrounding the paddock where the horses were grazing she was ready to admit she had actually followed her inclinations for once.

Climbing up a rung of the fence, she leaned her chin on her arms. Actually *living* life wasn't half bad, she reflected, tentatively examining her lips with the tip of her tongue, though perhaps in future she should spend a little more time thinking about the consequences of her actions before putting them into practice. Diego had turned the tables on her pretty comprehensively, leaving her lips with a swollen and throbbing reminder of how thoroughly she'd been kissed. Plus, he was right again, Maxie conceded with a rueful sigh. There was definitely passion lurking inside her somewhere.

'Now you've got that out of your system, are you ready for your first riding lesson?'

A lightning strike couldn't have shocked her more. Wheeling round, she took in Diego's dark, amused gaze at a glance. 'Riding lesson?'

'Unless you don't feel up to it?' he said, lips pressing down in a mocking reminder of her exhaustive assault on him.

She held the stare with a cool one of her own. 'I'm up to it,' she said, wishing the imprint of Diego's hands on her body hadn't left quite such a searing brand.

'I have just the horse for you,' he said, smiling pleasantly, which in itself was enough to make her suspicious.

'Would that be a stamping stallion to cart me off? Or a donkey?'

'You'll just have to rely on my judgement,' he said, and with one last amused look he vaulted the fence into the field.

Maxie studied Diego's powerful, athletic body as his easy stride ate up the distance across the field. Riding lessons had never been like this before. He returned with a mild grey pony and, tacking up, showed her how to hold the reins. Cupping his hands, he offered her a leg up. She was careful not to touch any part of him she didn't have to as she lowered herself gently onto the saddle.

'Are you listening, Maxie?' Diego demanded after they had been walking for a while.

'Of course I am.' She dragged her gaze from his wild, thick hair.

'Then loosen the reins,' he said impatiently.

She did so as she took in the wide sweep of his shoulders. Diego was such a big man. If a man that size made love to her would she enjoy it, or would he prove too big for her?

'Put your heels down,' Diego rapped in a voice that definitely suggested she had missed something. 'Aren't you listening to a word I say?' he demanded.

'I'm hanging on your every word,' she said solemnly, and for the pony's sake she would try. She was enjoying the gentle rocking movement of the horse—enjoying the chance to be close to Diego too, without the need for combat or conversation.

'You're a good pupil,' he remarked when he drew the pony to a halt.

'With an excellent teacher—even if he is a little impatient.'

Diego's glance sent heat streaking through her. She should know better than to challenge him. 'Well,' she said, turning in the saddle to gaze back at the house, 'I should be getting back.'

'I thought you said you had finished your work?'

'I have, but—'

'You have calls to take?' Diego suggested.

Warning signals flattened her enjoyment of the last hour. 'I'm due to ring Holly with a report,' she said quickly.

Diego released the pony into the field, and they were walking back to the house when he started to ask her more questions about her family. She didn't want to lie, but she wasn't going to betray her father's trust, either. 'There's just me and my father.'

'And that's it?' Diego pressed, frowning. 'No husband? No partner? No special boyfriend?'

She laughed. 'No one. Don't look so surprised. It works for me.'

'I think what you mean is it's all work for you,' Diego remarked dryly.

Just when she had relaxed into a laugh, he went on, 'So, no brothers or sisters, Maxie?'

'That's it,' she confirmed. 'You only think it's odd because you grew up in a crowd. What was that like, by the way?' she added, determined to steer the conversation away from herself.

'Noisy and chaotic.' Diego shrugged. 'Nacho brought us up. We gave him a hard time. No privacy—'

'No wonder you like it here,' she said. 'And it must have been fun when your friends came round—all this space?'

'Yes, it was,' Diego agreed gruffly. 'So what about your father, Maxie? Do you see a lot of him?'

'No,' she said quickly. Too fast. Alarm bells were ringing loud and clear now. Why the sudden interest in her father? She had done everything she could think of to protect his anonymity—booking him into a private nursing home under a different name where the staff was both loyal and discreet. 'Why are you so interested in my father?'

'Just curious.'

Her father's bungled business interests had never stretched to South America, of that much she was sure. He'd been ill for years, so he could never have met Diego—unless Diego had been just out of school.

'His name isn't Peter, is it?' Diego prompted lightly.

Maxie's heart stopped, and then began racing uncontrollably. 'No. Why?' That was not the name her father went under at the nursing home. She hated lying to Diego, but tell one person a secret and they told the next one, who told the next one, and in no time the whole world knew.

'I knew someone once with the surname Parrish,' he said with a dismissive shrug. 'That's all.'

'Common name,' she confirmed. She didn't know a lot about her father's business interests, other than to say he'd used to run a small and not very successful investment outfit. She couldn't imagine a wealthy South American from a polo playing family having anything to do with such a small-time broker, and it was a relief when Diego started to talk about a swimming machine for horses that strengthened their legs.

But just when she was relaxing into that topic he threw another curve ball. 'So you don't like talking about your home life, Maxie?'

'Only because there's nothing to tell...' Diego was way too perceptive, and she only now realised that her hands were clenched so tightly she was in danger of drawing blood from her palms.

When they got back to the house he made some excuse to put some space between them. He wanted to call his investigator. He had lots of gaps to fill in now.

'Thanks for the riding lesson,' Maxie said when they parted in the courtyard.

The blush in her cheeks suggested Maxie was remembering more than riding his horse. It made him keener than ever to find out the truth, and for his investigator to confirm that Maxie had nothing to do with Peter Parrish. She stood up to him like no other woman apart from his sister, and he liked that. He liked it a lot. In fact, Maxie Parrish was turning out to be the most intriguing and complex woman he had ever met.

If only he could bury the past once and for all...

He was confident Ruiz was right. There were countless people with the surname Parrish—and he hated the dark, twisted part of him that said nothing in life was ever that easy.

Diego's mouth firmed even as his heart lifted when Maxie walked into the kitchen that evening. He stared at her, hunting for something dark beneath those clear grey eyes, but there was nothing outwardly to suggest that Maxie might have any connection with Peter Parrish. He had still had no answers from his PI yet, but despite Ruiz's belief that the two were unrelated Diego still held a niggling doubt he could not explain.

'Good evening, Diego.'

'Good evening, Maxie...'

Putting down his newspaper, he registered the smell of

soap and some light scent she was wearing. Fresh jeans
and a long-sleeved white top made her look young, casual and relaxed. Her hair was still a little damp from the
shower, and the thought of burying his face in the silky
flesh above her shoulder was intoxicating. There were so
many ways he could put his dark thoughts behind him...

He settled for leaning back in his chair and putting
the first part of his plan into action. 'I imagine you have
plenty of work waiting for you in London?'

'Yes,' she said.

Actually, there was quite a gap in her schedule, Maxie
silently acknowledged. Not knowing what she would find
when she reached the island, she had built in some extra
time to allow for a change of venue had that proved necessary.

'Good.' Diego's lips pressed down with approval. 'I'm
very pleased to hear it.'

Was he? Something in Diego's voice wasn't quite right.
This thought was followed by a shiver of foreboding for
which she had no explanation.

'Supper,' he announced as Maria came bustling between them with steaming plates of hot food.

'Yes,' Maxie murmured, accepting everything was
indeed normal as she shook herself round.

He spent another restless night making plans. Keeping
Maxie close was number one on his agenda. He wanted
to know more about her, but he also acknowledged that
he wanted her in his bed.

Fortunately, Holly provided him with the perfect excuse when she rang him first thing. 'The charity event?'
he murmured, his mind racing as a plan began to take
shape in his head. 'Of course I haven't forgotten about
it.' Ideas were coming thick and fast now. 'Of course I'll

be home. I can't organise it from a distance, can I?' he said, dangling some tasty bait.

'But you know someone who can?' Holly prompted with a smile, supplying him with exactly the right cue.

'Do you mean Maxie?' he said, injecting surprise in his voice.

'Who else but Maxie?' Holly demanded, laughing at his apparent slowness to catch on.

'I suppose I could approach her...' He said this thoughtfully. 'We'll just have to hope she can work our charity event into her schedule.'

'If you ask her she will. I know she will. Please ask her, Diego!'

'All right,' he agreed indulgently. 'For you, I will.'

Maxie woke slowly and cautiously, and then groaned when she remembered everything that had happened the day before. Touching her lips before she had even opened her eyes, she hummed in rueful confirmation that they were still swollen, and that the area round them was still abraded where Diego's sharp black stubble had raked her skin. She reached for the pot of moisturiser by the side of her bed. She couldn't possibly afford an affair with Diego. She'd have to start buying face cream in bucketloads.

There was no chance she was going to have an affair with Diego, Maxie told herself firmly as she got out of bed. She was a realist, who was going to pack and get ready to go home.

Showering and dressing as fast as she could in T-shirt and jeans, she raced downstairs. A couple more photographs and one more report to the bride and she was done—out of here with her reputation more or less intact. By some miracle, Maxie concluded, as her body warmed just at the thought that Diego might be around.

Maria greeted her gaily with, *'Buenos dias, señorita.'*

'Buenos dias, Maria.'

'Señor Diego is waiting for you outside.'

'He is?' Maxie's heart began to thunder as she glanced out of the kitchen window.

'Your riding lesson,' Maria trilled.

'I thought I had one yesterday?'

'Practice makes perfect,' Maria assured her with a twinkling smile.

Maxie wasn't so sure about that. Grabbing a piece of toast and an apple, she paused to give Maria a hug. 'You're the best,' she said, giving the smiling house-keeper a squeeze before taking her concerns outside. Taking a deep breath, she steadied herself as she stared up at the man on the back of the impossibly fired-up stallion. 'Good morning, Diego.'

'Good morning, Maxie.'

Hmm. Something wasn't right here. Diego was hold-ing the mild grey pony on a lead rope at his side, while his mighty stallion pawed the ground and snorted imperi-ously. All right so far. It was just that look on his face—confident and...sexy. She laughed when the grey gelding turned a patient face towards her as if to say, *These guys are a pain, aren't they?*

'Yes, they are,' she said, stroking the grey pony's vel-vet muzzle.

'Who is what?" Diego demanded suspiciously as his stallion's bridle chinked an impatient warning.

'You don't need to know,' Maxie murmured, resting her cheek against the pony's warm, firm neck for a sooth-ing moment.

'Are you ready for your second lesson?'

'As I'll ever be,' Maxie agreed, wondering where this one would lead.

'Good. And I've got something else for you to consider.' Springing down, he looped the stallion's reins over his arm and helped her to mount up.

'Tell me?' she prompted once she was settled in the saddle.

'I've got another job for you—if you want it?'

She couldn't afford to turn work down. And she'd do almost anything to spend some more time with Diego, Maxie realised. Which was both dangerous and absurd.

'We hold a big charity event in Argentina every year at the *estancia*,' Diego explained as they started off down the path.

Maxie's mind automatically switched to business, and was soon filled with plans to ship things out to South America, along with the additional complication of sourcing dependable operatives without actually meeting them. *Argentina*...

'I take it you're pleased with my work?' She had to bat away seductive images of the wild pampas, and everything that went with it.

'Holly's very pleased with the work you've done here,' Diego explained. 'She's passed on that enthusiasm to the family. They want you to run things for us—as I do.'

'How can I help?' she said, desperately hanging on to a hank of mane as Diego urged their horses into a trot.

'Think Mardi Gras—parades, floats, stalls, fireworks and music…lots of music,' he called back over his shoulder, encouraging their horses to go faster.

'Mardi Gras is a little out of my range,' Maxie admitted hanging on for dear life.

'That's something that can be addressed, surely?' Diego countered.

'Can we slow down if we're going to discuss this? It's hard to talk when my teeth are clattering like castanets.'

'Of course,' Diego agreed with an amused look. 'Though all I need to know at this point is do you want the job or not, Maxie?'

'I'd love to pitch for it,' she admitted. With most of the loose ends tied up here, there *was* that gap in her schedule.

'I think you can take it you're the preferred supplier.'

'That's great.' She could hardly refuse another big job. 'I've just got one reservation.'

'Name it.'

'Will it include a polo match?'

'Of course.' Diego laughed. 'But we'll handle that. You just have to do everything else.'

'So, let me get this straight. You want me to arrange a charity event in Argentina the same way I've handled Holly's wedding—that is to say by e-mail and by phone?' She was already setting up the building blocks in her mind, Maxie realised. Apart from her personal concerns she would never refuse to help a worthy cause unless it was absolutely unavoidable.

'I was thinking of something rather more hands-on than that,' Diego admitted, slanting a look at her.

'Like what?' Maxie's antennae were already pinging warnings.

'You'd have to come to Argentina so you can see for yourself what has to be done.'

Her heart was banging in her chest, and it took her a jolting bounce or two before she was ready to speak. 'I'm afraid I can't,' she said then.

'Why not?' Diego demanded.

'Because my responsibilities keep me at home—I have a business to run.'

'Which you have proved you can run from anywhere in the world. Argentina is hardly as isolated as this island.'

And it *was* a great opportunity. So why did she feel that same shiver of apprehension, as if invisible walls were closing round her?

'You won't even have to sail a boat to get there,' Diego was telling her. 'I'll fly you there in the jet.'

'How exciting.' Under other circumstances she might have been overwhelmed by Diego's offer—but right now? She would be on his territory, and a long way from home.

But then he hit her with the clincher. 'Holly will be in Argentina at the same time as you, and as she travels the world with my brother this might be the only chance you two get to meet face to face before the wedding. My family needs you in Argentina, Maxie. And don't forget I need my therapist,' he added with a grin. 'Come on,' he pressed. 'Why the hesitation? Is it really so hard to visit Buenos Aires and the pampas *and* earn lots of money? You can't let us down,' he added, baiting her with his dark, intense stare. 'I've told my brothers all about your magic hands and they can't wait to meet you.'

Oh, great. The thought of meeting the Acostas *en masse* was daunting enough without that. Yes, but how many years of fees at the nursing home would a commission like this pay? Could she afford to refuse Diego's offer if it secured her father's future?

'You're making good progress with your riding,' Diego observed, forcing her back to full attention. 'I think you're safe to go a little faster.'

'No,' she exclaimed.

'Do you mean the riding or the event?' Diego called over his shoulder.

'I'm happy to accept the job,' she called back tensely.

'Excellent. I'm sure you won't disappoint us, Maxie.'

'I never accept a commission unless I'm sure I can exceed a client's expectations.'

But this time she might have bitten off more than she could chew, Maxie conceded when she saw the expression on Diego's face.

CHAPTER EIGHT

MAXIE felt as if the common sense she had lived by all her life was being jangled out of every one of her bones as her pony picked up speed to keep up with Diego's stallion.

'You'll find it easier if you move up and down like this,' Diego said as he demonstrated a rising trot. 'Keep it easy and relaxed, Maxie. Roll your hips like me.'

That settled it. 'I don't need to come to Argentina to do this job for you.'

'Of course you do,' Diego argued firmly.

'But I can organise everything from a distance,' Maxie protested. Accepting Diego's invitation would be madness, she realised, trying not to watch his muscular hips effortlessly thrusting back and forth.

'How can you possibly imagine the scale of the celebrations we're planning unless you come over?' he said.

True, Maxie conceded worriedly. So it would have to be a short visit—just long enough to take a look-see and get out with her heart intact. 'It shouldn't take me too long,' she mused out loud.

'Good. I'm glad that's settled,' Diego agreed.

'Can we slow down now?'

'I thought you liked speed?' Diego shouted back.

'I like control better,' she countered. And right now she was in danger of losing control of both the horse and her life. And that wasn't a situation she could allow to continue.

'Relax and it will all be fine,' Diego assured her, reining in alongside.

Was he talking about the horse or the charity event? But wasn't she a co-ordinator of fabulous events for other people to enjoy? This job in Argentina would take her business global, providing security for both Maxie and her father. She couldn't afford to turn it down. She'd call the nursing home as soon as they got back. Depending on the news on that front, she'd make a final decision. Caring for her father always posed a dilemma. If she didn't travel for her work she couldn't afford his fees at the nursing home, but when she travelled away from home she felt guilty.

'Stop dreaming, Maxie, and catch up.'

Diego had stopped beneath the sheltering canopy of a jacaranda tree. The frowzy purple blossom, dislodged by the wind, was drifting round him, creating a deceptively soft and dreamlike scene—but this was *business*, Maxie reminded herself as Diego explained that she would have the considerable weight of the Acosta name behind her in Argentina.

'I've done very well so far,' she said wryly, 'but I'd appreciate any help you can give me. A charity event on the scale you're proposing will need quite a bit of thinking about, and I want to check a few things before I give you my final answer.'

'Don't take too long,' Diego warned.

'Hey!' she protested, when he turned his horse and nudged it from a standstill into a canter and her horse followed.

'Have some confidence,' he called back. Maxie was a natural horsewoman. It was something in the hips. His lips tugged in a smile. He was enjoying this uncomplicated time together, but something told him it wouldn't last long.

The trip to Argentina went without a hitch. Maxie's contacts had been able to put her in touch with people in Buenos Aires, and the nursing home had given her the nod, so she was good to go. Diego had promised to introduce her to people who might be able to help her business further and was full of practical advice. There was no danger to her heart at all—which should have reassured her, but which left her with a niggling sense of regret.

The jet landed in brilliant sunshine, and her head was soon spinning with all the new sights and sounds. The thought of visiting not just Buenos Aires, the Paris of South America, but the pampas, with the most exciting man she had ever known, was exciting. She would soon grow accustomed to the seductive samba rhythms and the intoxicating scent of spice and heat and passion, Maxie reassured herself as Diego strolled towards a sleek black limousine.

So why the sense of doom approaching?

'Please excuse me, Maxie,' he said, fielding a call as they settled into the limousine with what seemed like acres of kidskin between them.

'No problem,' she murmured, knowing she would probably have to take quite a few business calls herself before they arrived at their destination.

One of the first things she noticed as they drove out of the airport was the colossal billboards lining the road. It was the first inkling she had of Diego's place in Argentina. The billboards featured the impossibly good-looking Acosta brothers. She recognised the groom, Ruiz, right away—smiling down with confidence. Diego's older brother, Nacho, appeared aloof. Kruz looked so laid back it was hard to imagine him in polo-warrior mode. And then there was Diego.

The same apprehension she'd felt when she got off the plane was back again, because Diego radiated danger. It was something in his eyes, Maxie concluded, glancing sideways at him. There were ghosts in Diego's life she couldn't begin to understand, and as theirs was a business relationship she could hardly ask him. He was still very much a mystery man, dangerously attractive and maybe dangerous to know. She wouldn't like to be his opponent on the polo field, or anywhere else for that matter, that was for sure.

'We'll be staying in Buenos Aires for a couple of nights,' he explained, stowing his phone. 'You'll get a chance to familiarise yourself with the city and with our usual suppliers. Then we'll travel to the *estancia* and you'll get the chance to see your first polo match. A friendly with Nero.'

Maxie laughed. 'Is there such a thing as a friendly polo match?'

Diego's mouth tugged fractionally. 'You'll soon find out.'

'Nero must be a good friend?'

'One of my closest. I trust him to tell me—'

Diego stopped and stared away, but she knew what he had been about to say. Nero would tell Diego if he was up to playing at international level. 'Either way it will be an important match,' she said.

'The most important,' Diego confirmed.

He didn't need to tell her that the chance to play at international level again meant everything to him. She knew as soon as he could after the accident Diego had been back on a horse, and he'd been training relentlessly ever since. His leg was so much better now she was sure he had nothing to worry about.

After they had been driving for a while he asked the driver to pull over. *'Empanadas,'* he said, pointing to a street stall. 'Delicious little savoury pastries,' he explained. 'You'll love them, Maxie. I'm starving. You must be too.'

'I'm always ready to eat,' she agreed with a smile. Diego was like a different man in Argentina. She should stop with the niggling doubts and make the most of this opportunity to do business with a man like no other. It would be something to hold on to when she went home to men with office pallor and perpetual sniffles, though she couldn't help wishing that Diego had shown some inclination to kiss her again.

She laughed when he bought up half the stall. 'This is crazy,' she said as he shrugged, but the tiny pastries were delicious, and it was fun being together and relaxed for a change. She was amazed by how quickly people recognised Diego, and autograph-hunters were soon clustering round. 'How do you cope?' she asked him when they got back in the car.

'I owe my success to these people,' he said, dipping his head to wave out of the window. 'I play to win for them.'

But when they drove off again, and a shadow crossed his face, she knew Diego was worrying that he might not live up to everyone's expectations. He was returning to polo after a long time out through injury.

'I'll work on your leg right up to the match,' she promised impulsively.

'I'm counting on it,' he said.

His dark, amused gaze made her heart thump like a jack-hammer. She was only doing a friend a favour, she reasoned, smoothing her jeans as an excuse to break eye contact. She had never risked getting too close to anyone, and she wasn't getting close now. None of her relationships had lasted—partly because she'd chosen the wrong men, but mostly because she had never forgotten the way her father had treated her mother. Yes, her father had changed when her mother had become ill, but it would have been nice for her mother to have had some happiness before that.

When Diego glanced at her, as if suspecting she was visiting some past regret, she only wished she could explain what she was thinking. But they weren't close enough for that—plus theirs was now a business relationship, and Diego had as many secrets as she did, Maxie suspected.

'We'll be staying at my apartment in the city,' he explained, providing a welcome distraction. 'You'll have your own suite of rooms, and can come and go as you like while you're in Buenos Aires.'

She had rather hoped Diego would show her round.

She pulled back when he suddenly wiped one firm thumb pad across the full swell of her bottom lip. 'Crumbs,' he explained.

The pastries, Maxie realised with embarrassment. 'Is that it? Or am I covered in crumbs?'

'I wouldn't know,' Diego murmured, his firm mouth tugging with amusement. 'I can only see those on your mouth.'

And now her face was burning. Diego had definitely relaxed since they'd landed. Was he intentionally turning up the heat?

Whatever was happening, she had to keep her feet on the ground. She had a job to do, and for all she knew Diego had a squad of girlfriends waiting in Buenos Aires

with another team on standby at the *estancia*. A man like
Diego Acosta would hardly be without a significant other.

An idea she should waste no time getting used to,
Maxie concluded when their limousine stopped at a junc-
tion and a group of young girls, spotting Diego, started
making remarks and frowning as they tried to work out
who he was with. Maxie couldn't blame them for dismissing her. In his blue jeans, dark jacket and crisp white
shirt, Diego looked like a film star—while if she was really lucky she might get a job sweeping the set. It was a
relief when they drove off again.

'Tell me how I can help you while you're here?' Diego
suggested, seemingly oblivious to all the attention.

Maxie thought for a moment before speaking. 'I'd like
you to give me a taste of Buenos Aires.'

'I'll try to give you more than you expect.'

That was what she was afraid of. 'Like what?' she
asked.

'I think you should wait and see. We'll drop our things
off at the apartment and then I'll take you into town and
you can pick up something special to wear tonight.'

'For what occasion?'

'Business, of course!' Diego laughed: a flash of white
teeth against his tan.

This sounded like business of a type she was unfamiliar with, Maxie concluded.

Diego's apartment in the best part of town was off-the-
scale fabulous. His penthouse occupied the entire top
floor of an elegant historic building. When they'd reached
it, in a private elevator with an ornate wrought-iron door,
they stepped out into an airy lobby with a domed ceil-
ing that wouldn't have looked out of place in the Vatican.
Grand double doors at one end of this spacious hall-

way had just been swung wide by a smiling middle-aged woman.

'My housekeeper, Adriana,' Diego explained.

Adriana ushered Maxie into a light-filled world, packed with sleek modern furniture and the latest high-tech gizmos. Very Diego, Maxie thought as she took in the striking décor of stark white walls punctuated by vivid flourishes of modern art. Floor-to-ceiling windows in the living room took in both the new and the venerably old buildings that comprised the exciting cityscape of Buenos Aires.

'This is stunning,' Maxie exclaimed, looking around.

'I call it home.'

'Lucky you.' Diego was so confident and overwhelming, while she was…overwhelmed. She took in the pale leather sofas, smoky glass tables, and the stainless steel conversation pieces at a glance. There was everything here a wealthy man might need. She was relieved to hear that Adriana lived on site, as she had no intention of becoming another of the home comforts Diego so obviously took for granted.

'Adriana will show you to your room,' Diego explained. 'Please make yourself at home, Maxie.'

It might take more than a single visit to feel at home in a place like this, Maxie concluded as the smiling housekeeper led her down a stylish corridor lined with discreetly framed pen and ink drawings of polo ponies.

The suite of rooms would easily have gobbled up Maxie's small house in London with room to spare. There was a large bedroom with a walk-in wardrobe, as well as a sitting room and a fantastic cream marble bathroom. She'd take a quick shower and then go shopping, Maxie decided. She had to make a start on filling those wardrobes—not to mention the shoe rack. Well, if she tried really hard she might actually manage to fill one small corner...

'Do you have everything you need?'

She whirled around to find Diego at the door. 'Are you kidding?'

'Good. I'll leave you to settle in and then I'll take you into town. See you in the hall in half an hour?'

'Thank you.'

She couldn't pretend the thought of going out with Diego didn't make her pulse race. She took a long, hot shower and then changed into casual clothes.

When Diego turned the corner into the hall and walked towards her she had to accept that seeing him never got any easier. Diego had also taken a shower, and his thick black hair was still damp and curled attractively around his face and neck.

'I hope I'm all right dressed like this,' she said, indicating her jeans and flat shoes. 'I wasn't sure what to expect, but I thought if I'd be walking—'

'You look great,' he said, barely glancing at her as he walked to the door.

Diego had a sister so he probably blanked out fashion questions as a matter of course, but Maxie wondered if she had underplayed it. Diego was wearing jeans and a crisp white shirt again, but he always looked outstanding, while she felt like a little grey mouse standing next to a tiger.

She might have known Diego would drive a bright red Ferrari. She might have known the moment he stepped out of the building he would be mobbed. She took refuge in the car, not wanting to be subjected to another trial of brief and dismissive scrutiny.

'You should stay with me,' he said when he joined her moments later. 'Why did you run off like that?' Closing the door, he gunned the engine. 'I could have used some support.'

It took her a moment before she realised he was serious. It had never occurred to her that someone like Diego might need anything in the way of a boost. 'I'll be there for you next time,' she promised wryly.

'Make sure you are,' he said, slanting a glance at her before lowering his sunglasses. 'That's why I love the pampas. It's such a contrast to the city. I can be anonymous there—unless we have a match, of course.'

'Tell me more,' she encouraged. This was such a contrast to the dark, brooding man who had met her off the boat, and she was curious about Diego's life before the accident.

'We never appreciated the space on the pampas when we were young. My sister Lucia, in particular, positively loathed it. She always felt she was missing out on everything that was happening in Buenos Aires. But now?' He shrugged. 'I guess Lucia feels as we all do that the *estancia* is both our sanctuary and a playground where we all relax. We have one of the best polo pitches in the country,' he confided, as if this might come as a surprise to her.

'I can't wait to see it,' Maxie said, thinking how frighteningly close she felt to him suddenly. How was she supposed to remain safely on the outside looking in now?

She didn't *have* to risk her heart, Maxie told herself sensibly. There was such a thing as friendship. They could just be friends.

CHAPTER NINE

WHEN Diego dropped her off, he explained to Maxie that she was on the most exclusive shopping street in Buenos Aires. She would be spoiled for choice, Maxie realised, wondering where to begin. How incredible was this? Maxie Parrish, a girl who arranged things for other people, was suddenly at the centre of all things up-scale and fabulous. And better still—thanks to the success of her business—she could afford it.

But Maxie soon discovered that money wasn't the problem. Being treated as if girls who wore jeans and sneakers couldn't afford to breathe the air on this exclusive street was. After trudging round every shop to no avail, she gave up. Spotting a market, she thought, why not? Buenos Aires wasn't known as the Paris of South America for nothing. The relaxed sprawl of colourful stalls reminded Maxie of the Left Bank markets in Paris. You never know…she thought, crossing the road to explore.

Fortune favours the brave, Maxie mused as she picked out a flirty dress and some sandals to go with it. She had wanted to buy a pair of simple flip-flops, but the young stallholder had wagged a finger at her and picked out a pair of sexy heels. Maxie felt like a baby stork when she tried them on, but the stallholder insisted she must have them.

'You'll be dancing on the street tonight,' she assured Maxie.

Maxie couldn't picture Diego dancing on the street—though she would like to, Maxie mused as she added a shawl to her purchases in case it grew chilly that evening. With her shopping expedition over, she rang Diego, who had promised to pick her up as soon as she called.

'Where are you?' he said, answering at the first ring. 'Alto Palermo? Avenida Santa Fe?'

'No—close to the market,' she explained, giving general directions.

'What?' he exploded.

'Don't fuss—I can have a coffee until you get here.'

'Don't fuss?' Diego roared. 'Like anywhere else in the world, some parts of the city are safer than others.'

'And this part is perfectly safe,' Maxie insisted. 'For goodness' sake, Diego, I'm not a child. I run a company—'

'And you are a visitor in a foreign land,' he flashed.

'Are you mistaking me for a woman who has lost her way, as all the assistants in those posh boutiques seemed to think I had?' Before directing her to what those shop assistants had explained would be a more affordable part of town, Maxie remembered angrily.

'What are you talking about?' Diego demanded.

'The assistants who refused to serve me just because I'm wearing jeans and sneakers?' she blazed back, wondering where all this passion had been hiding. 'I've told you where I am,' she flashed as anger and humiliation battled inside her, 'and I've told you I'm going to have a coffee.'

'*Dios,* Maxie!' Diego rapped down the phone. 'You'd better tell me which café. And where it is.'

She hadn't found one yet. She gazed around, searching for inspiration. 'Tortoni's?'

'Don't move a step. I'm coming for you!' Diego roared, nearly shattering her eardrum.

'See you in the café—' Maxie stared at the silent receiver in her hand. Diego hadn't even given her a chance to cut the line. But as she prepared to cross the road it occurred to her that it *was* rather nice to have someone to care about what she did. She hadn't had that since her mother had died. She could look after herself, of course, having done so for most of her life, but that didn't stop Diego's protective streak being a nice thing about him. But he was only concerned to hear she had strayed from the safety of the main shopping area, Maxie reasoned as she stared up at the façade of what appeared to be a popular café. Diego would feel that same sense of responsibility for all his employees. She only had to think about Maria and Adriana to know that.

As the door of the café opened she was greeted by a gust of warm air and the pungent smell of coffee. The noisy interior was full of men hunched over coffee cups as if the inky brew was the elixir of life, and families noisily sharing platters of food with all age groups represented, their happy faces reminding Maxie of so many mixed bouquets as they nodded their heads in time to the music.

And what music! The insistent throb of tango instantly invaded her veins. Couples were dancing between the tables, their gazes fixed on each other as they moved in a way she had never imagined could be so earthy and yet so sophisticated. She could hardly bear to blink in case she missed anything as the waitress showed her to a table.

Maxie was so enthralled by the dancing she allowed her coffee to go cold, and only snapped to at the sound of screeching brakes. This was swiftly followed by the slam of a car door, and she wasn't the only one staring at the entrance as Diego stormed in. Her breath caught in her throat as his glance swept the room.

'Maxie,' he growled, heading straight for her.

Diego nodded to a waiter, who quickly pulled out a chair.

'Hello, Diego.' Maxie tried to remain cool as her heart thundered nineteen to the dozen. How could anyone look so gorgeous? How could anyone carry such an air of command? It was enough to transfix every man and woman in the place, she noticed—but then Diego wasn't just a famous polo player, he was a frighteningly charismatic man, whom she guessed every woman wanted to go to bed with, and every man longed to call friend.

But he was hers.

Well, sort of, Maxie reasoned, trying not to give way to the waves of longing washing over her. She stared down in bewilderment at the crumbly little pastries on the plate in front of her, which the waiter had just put down without her ordering them.

'Eat,' Diego instructed. 'I'll watch your mouth.'

Trying to read Diego's thoughts was always a nonstarter. Was he teasing her, or was that a threat?

'Eat,' he repeated while she was still trying to work this out. And with that he turned away as if she was of no further interest to him.

'Excuse me, *señorita*?'

She glanced up to find one of the men who had been dancing the tango leaning over the table, trying to attract her attention. 'Yes?'

'You are not dancing?'

'No,' she agreed, wiping her mouth on her napkin.

'I would like to dance with you.'

Diego swung round so fast the table rocked. 'The *señorita* is with me,' he barked.

'Pardon, señor,' the man said with a bow, giving way.

Diego was interested now. He was so interested she couldn't say, 'I was going to refuse...' fast enough before he moved his chair back and stood up.

'You should have told me you wanted to dance, Maxie.'

'But I don't. In fact, I can't dance,' she explained.

'Why not?' Diego frowned.

Conscious that everyone in the café was staring at them now, she reduced her voice to an urgent whisper. 'I'm hardly dressed for it.'

Resting one strong hand on his tight hips, Diego scanned the room. All the couples dancing were dressed in everyday clothes, she noticed.

'Are you all out of excuses?' he demanded.

Not quite. 'I have two left feet.'

'Lucky for you I have one of each.'

Staring at Diego's outstretched hand, she pulled back in her chair. 'Seriously—I can't dance.'

'But I can.'

Which was how she found herself in the arms of a man she couldn't even look at without remembering how his kisses felt, or wondering what else he might be expert in.

'I find dancing is much improved if you move your feet,' he said, drawing her close. 'Just a suggestion, Maxie.'

'Of course.'

She would dance one dance with Diego and then sit down. There were so many people dancing between the tables that with any luck he would give up and she could start breathing evenly again. But somehow the dancers

managed to avoid each other, and Diego was more intuitive than most. Of course he was, Maxie reasoned,
fighting her body's best attempt to melt against him.
Diego was an international sportsman whose life re-
volved around second-guessing the competition. Now,
if she could just concentrate instead of being distracted
by erotic images bombarding her brain she might even
be able to move her feet in time to the music…

When the dance ended she was reluctant to leave
Diego's embrace. All the more reason to pull herself together, she concluded, heading back to the table. 'This
has been excellent research,' she informed him as he sat
down. 'I think we should have dancing at the charity
event.'

'Really?' Diego murmured. 'What an original idea.
Somehow I expected better of you, Maxie.' After a moment, he added, 'So, what did you buy to wear tonight?'

'I bought a dress in the market.'

He seemed surprised.

'It was pretty and I liked it. What's wrong with that?'

'Nothing,' he said. 'I'm just surprised you didn't find
anything in the shops where I dropped you off.'

She had no intention of reliving how embarrassing her
experience in the upscale part of town had been.

'Maxie?' Diego prompted.

'If you must know, I wasn't joking when I told you
they wouldn't serve me.'

'Honestly?' Diego sat back. 'I can't believe it.'

'Only because it would never happen to you.'

He frowned. 'But *why* wouldn't they serve you?'

'I'm not sure,' Maxie admitted. 'I can't think of anything other than the way I'm dressed.'

'Or maybe it's the slogan on your T-shirt?' Diego suggested, his dark eyes glittering. '"Drama Queen"? That's hardly you, is it, Maxie?'

'It's supposed to be ironic.' She lasted a moment and then began to laugh.

Diego wasn't smiling. 'The people in those shops need a wake-up call,' he said, standing up.

'Where are you going now?'

'To put a few people straight.'

'There are worse things in life than assistants who don't want to assist.'

'They are being paid to help customers find what they are looking for,' Diego argued, 'Even if that customer *is* a drama queen,' he added dryly. 'Come on,' he insisted, holding out his hand. 'I'm taking you shopping.'

Diego's approach to shopping was masculine and methodical, and while the usually meticulous Maxie would accept she was better known for her bemused dawdle when it came to choosing clothes, she was content to let Diego take the lead on this occasion. He was stopped every five minutes and asked for his autograph, which he always gave with a smile, good grace and a few kind words, and when they entered one of the high-class stores where Maxie had been ignored, far from seeing a shortage of assistants, they were mobbed.

'Just have everything sent over,' Diego stated on each occasion. 'My friend needs time to make her selection.'

Maxie's eyes widened. She did? Everything Diego had picked out looked fabulous to her, and there were mountains of clothes awaiting her perusal. He didn't even need to pay, because everyone knew him and said she could have the clothes on sale or return.

'The items the *señorita* has selected will be despatched

immediately by special courier,' they were assured in every shop.

And the clothes just kept on coming—shoes, bags, the most outrageous lingerie—and all of it would be waiting for them when they returned to the apartment.

'How can they be back before we are?' Maxie reasoned out loud when she remembered the speed at which Diego drove.

'If we beat them back we won't buy,' he said, and with such charm that the shop assistants were still swooning when they walked out of the shop.

'So that's how it's done,' Maxie remarked when they were back in the Ferrari. 'I should have taken you shopping with me in the first place.'

'I'm always available.'

Really? Somehow she doubted that. Maxie exhaled shakily as Diego removed the sunglasses from the top of his head and settled them in place. How far had she strayed from her businesslike brief now? 'You must tell me how much I owe you.'

'Nothing as yet.'

'But I have to pay my debts.'

'And I wouldn't have it any other way, *señorita,*' Diego assured her with a grin.

As he released the brake and eased into the evening traffic he couldn't remember enjoying himself so much for a long time. He couldn't bear injustice. Especially where Maxie was concerned, Diego realised, resting his chin on his arm when they got snarled up in traffic. He flexed his leg, which now felt better than ever. Who deserved spoiling more than Maxie? If it hadn't been for that Parrish shadow hanging over them…

'Problem?' she said when he frowned.

He relaxed back in his seat. 'Traffic.'

He was a simple man. All he asked was to be match-fit and for people to be honest with him. Trust was paramount to him. After the investment disaster trust mattered to him even more. Thinking back to the trust Nacho had placed in him, he realised he only associated with people he could rely on these days.

And Maxie?

He grimaced as he shifted position. Could he trust her? Who *was* Maxie Parrish? Who did he know who didn't talk about their family? What was she hiding? Maxie's explanation that he'd grown up in a crowd didn't wash. Surely everyone was proud of their family, even if they had one parent and no siblings. What was the difference? Family was family.

'You are preoccupied,' she remarked.

They had stopped in more traffic, which had given the old guilt plenty of time to wash over him. The more he enjoyed himself with Maxie, the more he remembered the friend who was dead—the friend who should be out with a girl now, having fun. The friend who should be laughing and loving instead of rotting in his grave—a grave Diego had helped to put him in. Peter Parrish had also played a part in it. No wonder he was preoccupied.

They drew to a halt outside his apartment, where men were already unloading their shopping parcels from a van.

'The driver must have broken every speed restriction in the book,' Maxie commented as they watched the stack of boxes wobbling their way to the entrance.

Lighten up, he told himself fiercely, realising he was grinding his jaw. 'Do you want me to report them for speeding?'

She laughed. When they had first met Maxie hadn't smiled, and neither had he. Her head had seemed to be occupied solely by business, while he had shut himself away like a dangerous animal. They'd both changed quite a lot since then. Wasn't this better?

'What?' she said.

He was staring at her, Diego realised. He wasn't about to tell Maxie where his thoughts had been. Whatever had happened in the past, maybe it was time to live a little. He gave an easy shrug. 'I was just thinking I'm looking forward to tonight.'

'Me too,' she said lightly.

But he couldn't remember ever wanting to spend an evening with a woman quite so much.

She had only opened a fraction of the packages stacked neatly in the dressing room of her suite. It looked as if Christmas and her birthday had come together times ten. 'I've got an idea,' she said later, when they were sipping coffee in Diego's office where she had made a start on her work.

'Tell me,' he prompted.

The coffee cup hovering a hair's breadth from Diego's sexy lips held her up for a moment. 'We tell the stores we've visited today about your charity and choose a few of the things from the selection of clothes delivered we think might sell well. It's such a high-profile charity, and with the Acosta name attached…'

'It would be excellent publicity for all involved? I hope you're right.'

'I am,' Maxie said confidently.

'Then go with it. How do you propose to sell the items? An auction?'

'A Dutch auction,' Maxie explained, growing in enthusiasm. 'I've run one before and it was a huge success. The donated goods are displayed and people put sealed bids on anything that takes their fancy. I think we could raise a lot of money—'

'You're full of good ideas,' Diego interrupted, 'but when are you going to fit this one in?'

'I'll get everything sorted out before we leave for the *estancia*. That's what phones are for—and the internet,' she mocked as she glanced at his desk.

Having made a point of telling her she could work from anywhere, he could hardly disagree. 'Good to know you won't be slacking while you're here.'

'Oh, don't worry. I won't be.'

'I was joking, Maxie. There's only one other person I know who's as dedicated to their work as you.' It was his turn to glance at the desk, where six monitor screens were winking.

'We make a good pair—I mean...'

'I know what you mean,' he assured her as her cheeks fired up. 'Well,' he said, standing up and stretching, 'I'm going to get ready.'

'You haven't said where we're going yet.'

'Just wear that dress from the market—it's the prettiest, isn't it?'

'I'm surprised you noticed.'

'I notice everything.'

Was he joking now? she wondered as Diego's smile made more than her cheeks heat up.

She waited for him in the kitchen. This was just another research opportunity, right? Perhaps if she told herself that enough she would believe it...

Nope. That didn't work. Her heart didn't believe it and neither did her body. And when Diego walked into the kitchen her bedazzled eyes didn't believe it either. Just for a change he looked amazing. Close-fitting jeans and a tight-fitting top with desert boots was all it took to do that. It was the way the clothes clung to Diego's powerful frame, Maxie decided, that made him so sexy.

'Are you ready?' he prompted, dipping his head to stare into her eyes.

'Absolutely,' she confirmed, hoping she sounded more businesslike than she felt.

And then her phone rang.

'England?' Diego murmured as she covered the mouthpiece.

'Work,' she said. Of course it wasn't work. She hated lying to Diego as much as she hated staring into her father's heart-wrenchingly blank eyes, but no one was going to find Peter Parrish through *her*.

Her father was ranting again. Moving out of earshot, she tried to soothe him. 'I'm sure it will be all right. Have you taken your medicine today?' She was whispering and trying to act as if this was a business call. 'I see,' she said, practically swooning with relief when a nurse rescued the phone and was able to assure her that everything was in hand.

'Are you ready to go now?' Diego asked as she ended the call.

'Yes.'

'Come on, then.'

She glanced up to find Diego smiling faintly, but his eyes betrayed the calculation behind them. That shadow crossed her path again, and she had to reassure herself quickly that this evening was just research for work— and, anyway, what could she possibly do to upset Diego?

She heard the music first—or rather the drum beat. Rhythmical and deep, it was unashamedly primal and had drawn people from all quarters of the city. There was no point taking the car, Diego had explained, as most of the roads were blocked off for the carnival procession. Maxie didn't mind at all. It was fun walking with the high-spirited *portenos,* as the city-dwellers were known, pretending she was one of them. Take that fantasy to the next level and she could imagine they were a couple—or she might have done had there not been a yawning gap of a couple of yards between herself and Diego.

'Hey,' he said, pulling her close when they were briefly separated by a group of people.

The fantasy was back on track, but it would have been better if Diego's sexy vibes were heading her way, instead of him just having to grab hold of her to stop her getting lost in the crowd.

He enjoyed holding Maxie's hand. But he wanted more than that. He wanted to make love to her. He wanted to find out if those calm grey eyes would fire with passion as they had when she'd kissed him...

'Carnival?' she said, distracting him. 'That's the theme you want for the charity event?'

'Hardly original,' Diego agreed. 'But there's something for everyone and it works every time.' He should be glad Maxie had pulled him back to business, but after that phone call—after *all* those mysterious phone calls— he wanted to drill everything out of her. Although if he pushed too hard he knew she would retreat back into her shell.

They were entering a large square where competing groups of musicians were trying to make as much noise as they could.

'Carnival can be dangerously overheated,' he yelled in her ear, 'so stay close to me.'

Oh, no. She should be concentrating on how to adapt this city-sized carnival to something on a suitable scale for the Acosta event—not thinking about Diego's minty breath on her ear.

'What do you think so far, Maxie?' he shouted above the noise.

'Like I've only ever worked in monochrome before,' she admitted, making a grateful return to business mode. 'If I can capture all this—' She gestured around.

'You will,' Diego yelled confidently, locking his strong arm even more tightly around her shoulders as they got jostled. 'But no more business tonight—tonight is fiesta. Once a year we can forget about everything and just let go.'

That was what she was afraid of. There was danger behind Diego's laughing eyes, and she had too many secrets to let herself go, as he suggested. In fact it was time to move away from the danger zone. The crowd was so dense now they were locked together like lovers. Diego glanced down. Their stares met and held and it was the most natural thing on earth when he kissed her.

There was nothing *natural* about it. Diego was her employer and she was here on business. Purely business, she told herself, slowly melting.

'Have you seen enough?' he murmured, nuzzling his mouth against her lips. 'Is there some more research you feel you should do?'

'No.'

'Do you think we'll make it back to the apartment?' he murmured, smiling against her mouth.

'We can only try.'

Locking his arm around her shoulders, Diego led her swiftly away.

CHAPTER TEN

THEY ran laughing into the apartment. Slamming the door behind them, Diego leaned back against it and dragged her into his arms. 'I've wanted this since the first moment we met…'

'Liar.' Locking her hands behind Diego's neck, she threw up a challenging stare. 'I haven't forgotten your face when you stood on the dock watching me berth that boat.'

'Will I ever forget?'

'Brute!'

'Sloppy sailor.'

'Savage.'

Diego stopped her talking with a kiss. 'I should have done that a long time ago,' he said, swinging her into his arms.

Carrying her into the bedroom, he kicked the door shut behind them and lowered her to the ground in front of him. She held her breath as he slowly slid the shoestring straps of her dress from her shoulders, never once taking his eyes from her. The sliver of silk fell to the floor, revealing the racy lingerie Diego had chosen for her in all its insubstantial glory.

'Very nice,' he murmured approvingly.

'I'm glad you like it,' she said, realising that Diego

gave her confidence as he dropped kisses on her shoulders and on her neck, and made her shiver with desire when he whispered outrageous things in her ear. He made her laugh until she cried and begged him for more. 'You'd better not stop this time,' she warned, teasing his bottom lip with her teeth.

'You're very forward, Señorita Parrish…'

Yes, she was—incredibly. Maybe because something deep deep down told her this was going to be different. Because Diego was different. She had waited a long time for this and she wasn't about to play the shrinking violet.

'You're overdressed,' she said, shivering with nerves and anticipation.

Diego had no inhibitions, and tugged off his top without a word.

'Shameless,' she whispered, filling her eyes with his incredible form as she trembled with sexual excitement. He was so big. And those sexy tattoos… 'Your belt?' she prompted.

'Whatever you say…' Releasing it, he let it hang. Undoing his jeans, he dropped them and kicked them away. 'Boots?' he suggested.

'Not a bad idea,' she agreed, loving the fact they shared the same humour.

'We made it to the apartment,' he commented. 'What are our chances of making it to the bed?'

That was clearly not a serious question as Diego didn't wait for her to answer. Swinging her into his arms, he carried her over to the bed and set her down gently on top of it. Stretching out beside her, he made her pulse rage out of control. His earring flashed in a beam of light stolen from the hallway, and as she stared into his sleepy black tiger eyes he seemed more a creature of the night than ever. The width of his shoulders was deliciously intimidating. The power and promise in his muscular, deeply tanned body stormed her brain with erotic thoughts. By the time he took hold of her in a grip so light she could have broken free at any time she was on fire for him, but Diego made no move to drag her close. He was waiting for her to come to him, she realised when she read his eyes. That was the deal. That was Diego's deal.

He had never wanted a woman more, and had to smile when Maxie, in her typical up-front way, felt she had to explain to him that her experience in the bedroom was below average, but not non-existent.

'Thank you for being so frank with me,' he said, adopting the same serious tone, though he couldn't quite keep the smile from tugging at his lips.

'Are you disappointed with me?' she said, moving restlessly in his arms.

'Disappointed about what?' he asked, brushing his lips across her mouth when he wasn't teasing her lips with his tongue.

'That I'm not a virgin and I'm not an expert either?'

'Let me think,' he replied. 'Hmm. No. I just want to kiss you again.'

'This isn't fair,' she complained when he released her. 'I know nothing about your experience. Okay,' she said quickly, 'I don't want to know.'

He kissed her again. Over and over. He was hungry, but he held back, knowing Maxie had been disappointed in the past and probably expected the worst now. Everything was by the book for Maxie, and she had been reading too conservatively. It made him more determined than ever that she was going to remember tonight for all the right reasons.

She had never imagined Diego could be so gentle, so

caring, or so controlled, or that his murmured promises could both reassure and excite her. They had run into the apartment like two storm fronts meeting, but this was better, she realised as he slowly undressed her.

'Patience,' he murmured, working some magic with his hands when she angled her body to show how much she wanted him.

'Don't make me wait too long,' she warned shakily as Diego kissed a leisurely path across her neck and on over her chest. His hands knew just where to touch, and promised more pleasure than she had ever known. Closing her eyes, she indulged herself by exploring Diego's extraordinary physique, but when she felt the size of his erection pressing against her she sucked in a nervous breath.

'Relax' he murmured, adding some more suggestions to excite her.

'Is that even possible?'

'Why don't we find out?' he said with a kiss.

She parted her lips under the pressure of his tongue, and as Diego's kisses grew more heated so her own hungry demands grew. He suckled her nipples through the cobweb-fine lace of her bra then, opening the catch, he pulled it off and tossed it aside. Breath shivered out of her as he made a light pass with his stubble-blackened chin across the sensitive peaks, and he drew another soft moan of need when he moved his attentions to her belly. She was trembling uncontrollably now, but Diego continued teasing and stroking as she writhed helplessly beneath him.

It wasn't until his fingers found the most needy part of her that she went still. She wasn't going to move a muscle to distract her mind from the most amazing sensation she had ever known, and as if knowing this Diego held her firmly in place, forcing her to enjoy everything he wanted to do to her. It was a relief when he stripped her flimsy thong away, and when he pressed her thighs wide she doubted she would survive the pleasure. But she was going to have the best time ever struggling for survival, she realised when Diego buried his face deep.

She hadn't expected such a big man to be capable of such finesse, or to be so intuitive, Maxie realised. Had she really thought Diego would be too strong for her— too big, too quick, too passionate, too frighteningly intense? He was the most skilful lover. He didn't make her feel as if she was in a race, but gave her all the time in the world to lie back and drown in pleasure. He was wholly…rhythmically…dependably…focussed on satisfying her most outrageous desires.

Too much so, she realised suddenly with alarm, realising she couldn't hold on.

When Maxie fell she fell *big,* Diego realised as her hips worked furiously beneath his hands. He made sure she enjoyed every moment, and when she quietened he held her in his arms until she was calm again, kissing and stroking her as he soothed her. When she could focus on his face she laughed—softly, sexily. It was the most intimate moment he could remember sharing with anyone, and he couldn't have anticipated the rush of emotion he felt when he gathered her in his arms. Just for once he was going to let the name Parrish mean something *good* to him. How could he not, when Maxie had done so much for him? This woman hadn't just healed his leg she had given him his life back. He laughed softly when she wanted more, and whispered some more suggestions to make her gasp.

'Please,' she whispered urgently.

He had never experienced this level of feeling before, he realised as he protected them both. Maxie was swollen and moist and ready for him, but still he took her gently, testing and teasing by withdrawing completely after giving her just the tip. Predictably, she told him off for that. She couldn't know it was taking all he'd got to hold back. And she *wouldn't* know, he determined as he pressed her knees back. Sinking into her silky, welcoming warmth, he knew he was stretching her, and so he caressed her delicately and rhythmically, both to reassure and to please her all the more.

'Yes?' he murmured.

'Yes,' she groaned, pressing her thighs open for him.

The only reward he wanted was to see pleasure in her eyes. She didn't disappoint. He kept her suspended on a plateau with only one way down, and a single word was all it took. *'Now,'* he murmured against her mouth. Exclaiming with relief, she stabbed her fingers into his buttocks and drove him on, until violent spasms claimed her and left her gasping in their wake.

She slept in his arms, and when she stirred he couldn't have been more surprised as she reached for him. 'You've been having things far too much your own way,' she complained groggily, with barely enough strength to open her eyes.

'Explain,' he whispered, dropping kisses on her face as he stroked her hair.

'I think you need putting in your place, *señor.*'

'Please,' he said wryly, resting back when she moved over him. And now it was his turn to suck in a ragged breath as Maxie began to kiss her way down his chest and on across the banded muscles of his belly. It wasn't often his muscles trembled like this, but when her sharp teeth nipped at him and her hot tongue worked with such purpose he realised Maxie had taken to lovemaking with the same enthusiasm she showed in every other area of her life.

'Why are you laughing?' she demanded, lifting her head.

'I'm enjoying myself.'

'The feeling's mutual,' she assured him. 'What?' she said when his expression changed.

'You,' he admitted. Reaching up, he swung her beneath him. 'I like being with you.'

'I like being with you too.'

He laughed. They were both so guarded they deserved each other. He kissed her again, and that kiss deepened into something that bound them. Moving over her, he took her slowly and with more care than ever. He was so much bigger than she was, brutish after years of training, while Maxie was small, and for all her bravado vulnerable, and the last thing he wanted to do was to hurt or frighten her in any way.

She felt so safe with Diego, even when their hunger for each other burned white-hot. It pleased her to pleasure him, and when he groaned and threw his head back she teased him with feather touches that made him exclaim with pleasure. When she mounted him and eased herself steadily down it was the most natural thing in the world to move her hips languorously back and forth.

You don't need lessons for this, she thought wryly when Diego suggested, 'More?'

'Oh, yes, I think so,' she agreed, as his strong hands took control of her buttocks.

Neither of them could hold on, and the ending left them both exclaiming with surprise.

When she was calm again Diego drew her into his arms. Cupping her face in his hands, he kissed her in a way that made her eyes sting. The passion between them couldn't have been hotter, or his kisses more cherishing as she fell asleep.

He watched over her as she slept. Her dark hair was spread like a smoky cloud across his pillows, while her eyelashes created crescent shadows on the flawless bloom of her cheeks. He wanted to kiss her slightly parted lips, but he didn't want to wake her. She was breathing steadily and sighing from time to time, as if she had never been more content. He could stare at her all night. It was hard to believe he could fall so completely for a woman about whom he knew practically nothing!

What if...?

He moved his head from side to side on the pillow, as if that could dislodge the doubts. Maxie couldn't be part of that terrible time. It was unthinkable that he could be lying here with the daughter of the man who had caused the death of his closest friend...

Yes, Oresto was dead—and Diego was responsible. His closest friend—a man he had known from childhood—and nothing would bring him back. Not this self-flagellation, that was for sure. His guilt wouldn't soften the grief for Oresto's family, and Diego must accept what couldn't be changed or he would damage even more people, he realised, gazing at Maxie.

She sat up in bed, instantly awake the moment the light of a new day hit the window. She could hear Diego in the bathroom, shaving and cursing. He sounded in an extremely good mood, Maxie thought as he came back into the bedroom, wiping his face on a towel.

'You're awake,' he said. Dropping the towel, he launched himself onto the bed. She screamed with laughter and embraced him.

'You're crazy—do you know that?' she demanded, covering him in kisses.

'Good morning, Señorita Parrish,' Diego said, returning her kisses with interest. 'I trust you slept well?'

'I would have done, but this man kept me awake all night,' she said, frowning.

'No. Really? Where is he?' Diego demanded, glancing fiercely round the room. 'Let me kill him so my honour is satisfied.'

'I think your honour is very satisfied,' she observed, happily stretching.

And then her phone rang.

In the space of one strident peal, that carefree mood—her sense of completeness, togetherness, of sharing everything they were and had between them—shattered into tiny, ugly pieces.

'You'd better answer it,' Diego said, moving away to give her some privacy.

'Sorry,' she said, holding the phone to her chest until he was out of earshot. Winding the sheet round her body she rushed across the room to the window, where the reception was good and there was no chance Diego could hear her. She glanced at him with more apologies ready on her lips.

'Go ahead,' he said without expression. 'I'll get dressed.'

'Your father has a small infection,' the nurse was saying while Maxie stared at the empty space left by Diego. 'But you should be fine to continue your business trip,' the nurse added, 'so enjoy it while you can.'

Maxie's heart sank at the implied warning, and sank again when she thought what it meant for her tender new relationship with Diego. 'You'll let me know if anything changes?' she urged, already feeling the ice of loss creeping through her veins.

'Of course,' the nurse assured her briskly.

Maxie stood still for a moment when she had ended the call. She'd seen the expression on Diego's face. Goodness knew who he thought was ringing her at this time in the morning. How was she going to answer his questions? She couldn't lie to him. She couldn't pretend it was a business call. Since sleeping together something had changed between them. They had placed their trust in each other. Was she going to break that trust now?

She didn't have to say anything unless Diego brought it up, Maxie reasoned. This was her problem and she would sort it out. She just had to hope there would be time to finalise everything for the charity event before her father's condition worsened.

'Problem?' Diego asked, towelling his hair.

'Nothing I can't handle.' Did her voice sound as false to him as it did to her?

'Are you sure?'

'I'm certain.'

'That's good,' he said, tossing his towel onto a chair, 'because I've got news for you. While you were on the phone I took a call from my brother. We're leaving for the *estancia* today.'

'Today?'

'Do you have a problem with that?'

'No, of course not.' She would be moving further away from her father, but one step closer to finishing the job. Which meant she would be leaving Argentina and Diego for good. 'Great,' she said, forcing a smile.

No man was in for the long haul, Maxie reminded herself, not unless guilt held him close, she realised, with her mother's experience clear in her mind. And she wanted more than that. Perhaps it was as well she would be leaving soon.

Diego explained their travel plans and seemed more concerned about her meeting his family than the mysterious phone calls she'd been taking. 'I can't wait to meet them,' she said, thinking he had become a little reserved on the subject.

'You may not see too much of me,' he explained in a way that chilled her, 'as I will be preparing for the match when we reach the *estancia*.'

'I wouldn't expect anything else,' she assured him. Walking across the room, she rested her face against his chest. 'I know how much this first match means to you.'

'I wouldn't be playing at all if it wasn't for you.'

But there was chill in his voice, as if mentally he was pulling back. Even the arms that had held her so securely felt mechanical, somehow. 'I'll do anything I can to help you,' she said, 'and please don't worry about me when we arrive at the *estancia*,' she added, hoping that by teasing Diego she would restore his former good mood. 'I'll be so busy there's no chance I'll get in your way. So you'd better not get in mine.'

There was a pause, and then he responded as she had hoped he would. 'I'll still need my therapist,' he said, in the warm tone that could sometimes be frighteningly elusive.

'As I will need mine,' she assured him.

Diego's kiss was long and deep, and when he pulled his head back to look at her there was something in his eyes that should have filled her with all the reassurance in the world. But it vanished quickly. 'Well, we'd better get on,' he said briskly. 'I imagine you have packing to do?'

'Yes, I have,' she said, knowing that nothing this good ever lasted.

She should also remember that Diego had shadows too, Maxie reminded herself. Let him get this first match out of the way, and then she would tell him about her father and there would be no more secrets between them.

CHAPTER ELEVEN

THE flight from Buenos Aires to the airstrip at Estancia Acosta took no time at all with Diego at the controls, but the intimate look they'd shared when Diego secured her seat belt before returning to the cockpit made any separation far too long. It would be so easy to get used to having him around, Maxie reflected, and that was foolish.

The jet landed lightly on a bleached strip of sand set like a golden ribbon on a plain of richly coloured flatlands. The airstrip was empty other than their jet and a solitary truck, beside which stood a traditionally dressed Argentinian cowboy. A *gaucho,* she realised, breaking free of her concerns. She had finally arrived on the pampas.

Their jolting journey to the *estancia* was a great introduction to the local scenery. Diego sat up front while Maxie leaned out of the open window, letting the warm breeze mess with her hair and her senses fill with the scent of ripe corn and lush green grass. Everything was on such a vast scale—from the huge skies to the seemingly endless grasslands that stretched away to the misty purple horizon. The flat land was punctuated by paddocks populated with herds of wild horses, and there were more ponies clustering by the fence as they approached the towering gates of the Acosta family home, which loomed out of the ocean of grass like the entrance to some Wild West ranch.

The moment they drove up to the front door people poured out, and when she climbed down from the truck Maxie was engulfed in a whirlwind of warm-hearted greetings. Diego was at her side throughout, though to her disappointment he insisted it was too soon for lengthy introductions as Maxie was tired from their journey. It was almost as if he didn't want her to meet his family properly, she thought as everyone said they understood, and agreed that Maxie must retire to her suite of rooms and that a dinner tray should be sent up.

'What a wonderful family you have,' she exclaimed as Diego escorted her into the house.

'I'm pleased you think so,' he said, with that same chill note. 'They certainly took to you.'

Was that a criticism? she wondered, trying to read him.

'I'll see you in the morning,' he said as the house-keeper loomed. 'I'll be in my old room, if you need me.' Her heart shrank a little more when Diego added in the same cordial tone, 'Don't set an alarm—sleep in for as long as you like.'

It was almost as if he didn't want her to spend time with his family, when she wanted to be up with the lark so she could get to know everyone. And she hadn't planned on sleeping alone.

She should stop being unreasonable and realise that now Diego was home he probably didn't want everyone knowing they were having such a passionate affair. What did she think this was? Meet the family prior to an announcement? She was here on business—or had she forgotten that?

* * *

Diego ground his jaw as he walked to the stables. The suspicions were back. There was still no news from his PI, so he had no way of knowing if Maxie was involved with Peter Parrish. Yet he had brought her to his family home—to the house where he had used to play with Oresto when they were children—a house that held so many treasured memories. His family had welcomed her with open arms—no suspicions. There was only Diego wondering why Maxie looked so very pleased to be here. Why so pleased? Was she on a scouting mission so she could report back to Peter Parrish?

Now he was being ridiculous, Diego accepted. Maxie was a welcome guest who had been employed to do a very important job for the Acosta family. She would not be reporting back to some unseen enemy. It was he who was out of step.

She took a bath in the comfortable old-fashioned bathroom, trying not to feel too disappointed. But she hadn't expected the break with Diego to be so sudden, nor that he would usher her away from his family as if he was ashamed of her. She would handle it the only way she could, Maxie concluded—she'd do her job and she'd do it well. She had to meet Holly, the bride-to-be, tomorrow. So however Diego wanted to play it there was only one game plan for Maxie, and that was to be the best guest she could be as she finalised all the arrangements with which she had been entrusted.

It had been such a confusing day, with such a multitude of new things to take in, that Maxie had expected to stay awake worrying half the night, but once she slipped beneath the starched white linen sheets she was asleep within minutes.

Everything looked better in the morning. Far from

sleeping in, as Diego had suggested, she threw back the curtains at dawn. The ranch had come alive at first light. She could hear people banging around in the kitchen, and she couldn't wait to get down there and see everyone.

She showered and dressed, and then booted up her laptop to check her mail. The stores were on board with her idea for an auction, which was great. It was all systems go for the charity event, at least. Closing the computer down, she left the room and ran downstairs to find Lucia and Holly waiting for her in the hall. Within minutes it was as if they had known each other all their lives.

'Well, we do have rather a lot in common,' Maxie pointed out when Lucia commented on this.

'Yes,' Lucia agreed wryly. 'Wild men of the pampas.'

'I wouldn't put it quite like that,' Maxie argued, laughing even as she wished this was true.

'Well, I would!' Holly said, hugging Maxie impulsively. 'I couldn't be more pleased to meet my wedding planner at last.'

Lucia smiled. 'And those wild men haven't been accountable to anyone in their lives. It's about time we brought them into line. We will welcome your input, Maxie.'

'Me?' Maxie exclaimed, knowing she'd better get a few things straight. 'When I said we have a lot in common, I was thinking about the work I'm doing here for the charity event and for your wedding, Holly.'

But the two girls refused to go along with this. 'And I suppose Diego has nothing to do with it at all?' Lucia said, exchanging an amused glance with Holly.

This was how close friendships started, Maxie thought. She didn't have the heart to tell the girls that where Diego was concerned their excitement was completely misplaced.

* * *

The next week flew by, with Maxie constantly working on her phone or on her laptop, contacting suppliers and putting things in place for the charity event as well as tying up the last few loose ends for Holly's forthcoming wedding. Diego was busy too, both with his training and with the many business meetings he held each day with his brothers. More importantly, he seemed to have relaxed into the idea of Maxie being part of the family, for however short a time, and though there was still something there she couldn't put her finger on they hadn't been able to stay apart for very long.

She felt at home, Maxie realised, gazing out across the paddock from her bedroom window. Shadows were lengthening as the bleaching light of day gave way to a soft lilac dusk, but the brothers were still training tirelessly for the forthcoming match. Diego glanced up, as if he sensed her staring at him. She knew that look, and her body responded along with her heart.

Springing down from his horse, Diego handed the reins to one of his brothers and, vaulting the fence, came towards the house. Hugging herself, she pulled back from the window.

She stood with her back to the door, trembling with anticipation, when Diego walked in. Walking up behind her, he kissed her neck as he pushed the robe she had flung on after her shower from her shoulders. She was naked beneath it. No words were spoken. None were needed. Diego lifted her so she could lock her legs around his waist. Throwing her head back as he entered her, she let the pleasure come. Diego was so strong and sure, and she was always so hungry for him. There was no finesse today. This was a storm of passion as they rode towards a horizon they had never failed to reach. Holding her firmly in place, as he thrust steadily at the tempo he knew she liked, he took her strong and deep, with the type of stroke that always brought her quickly to the edge. She didn't even think of holding back and tumbled gratefully, bucking furiously until the storm had passed and she rested spent in his arms, while her muscles throbbed a powerful reminder in the aftermath of pleasure.

'Do you think we should take this to bed?' Diego suggested wryly.

'Only if you allowed me to undress you,' she whispered.

Rolling back his handsome head, Diego smiled. 'I'm already undressed,' he pointed out.

'That's where you're wrong,' she said, lifting his top out of his tight-fitting breeches. Standing on tiptoe, she tugged it over his head, revealing the magnificent torso that always excited her—especially now, when his muscles were pumped and defined after exercise. The breeches were next. They clung to him like a second skin, outlining the evidence of both Diego's stamina and his size. 'Are you never at rest?' she said, cupping her hands around him.

He shrugged, which made her smile.

'Why are you smiling?' Diego murmured speculatively.

'I have no intention of stroking your ego when it clearly doesn't need any more attention,' she said.

'You're right. Please don't waste time stroking my ego,' he said as he kicked his breeches away. 'Bed?' he suggested. 'I think that's a much better option, don't you?'

Before she could answer this Diego had lifted her and put her down on the bed. Turning her, he took her gently, rocking her back and forth, while she sighed with pleasure. She was so receptive, so incredibly sensitive;

it seemed the more they made love the more she wanted Diego, and the more responsive she became. He was such an unselfish lover. There wasn't a part of her he hadn't pleasured or a request he hadn't fulfilled.

'Now,' she murmured in the way he had taught her, angling herself shamelessly and gasping with excitement as his grip tightened on her buttocks. He was so good at this. Clutching the pillow as sensation grew beyond the point of bearing, she cried out, 'I can't—it's too big—too strong—' Thankfully, Diego ignored her and, screaming wildly, she had the satisfaction of feeling him fall with her in a frenzy of explosive pleasure and release.

Could anything be more perfect than this? Maxie wondered as she pulled on some clothes after her shower. Even if she must go home soon, at least she had tasted life to the full.

Diego had returned to his training. His brothers had accepted him back in the floodlit arena as if a bedroom break in the middle of training was a perfectly natural thing.

Everything about this visit had exceeded her expectations, Maxie realised. Diego was…Diego. While the job was going even better than she had anticipated. Her career was thriving, thanks to the associated publicity, and a huge bonus to all this was the relationships she had formed with Lucia and Holly. She had particularly enjoyed hearing Lucia's stories about Diego.

'He needs someone like you to take him out of himself,' Lucia had confided. 'Diego can become very insular at times. He shuts us out—like the time he went to Isla del Fuego to recover from his injuries, allowing none of us to help him.'

Maxie had wondered about this, and had asked, 'Has he done that sort of thing before?'

Lucia's face had creased with concern and, not wanting to pry, Maxie had quickly changed the subject. Spotting Lucia in the courtyard now, she waved out of the window to attract her friend's attention, yelling that she would be right down.

Lucia greeted her with a hug. 'It's so good to have female company,' she said, glancing at the paddock. 'Come on—let's go and see what they're doing.' Linking arms with Maxie, she drew her towards the training field, where the men were shouting at each other as they wheeled their horses at impossible angles and galloped back and forth. 'I love them all dearly,' Lucia confided, 'but they can be a little overpowering.'

'I can imagine,' Maxie agreed wryly. 'I can't think what it must have been like for you growing up in a household of such strong-minded men.'

'Hell,' Lucia assured her. 'They wouldn't let me tie my own shoelaces in case I tripped over them. But now there's Holly—and you.'

'But I won't be staying,' Maxie pointed out.

'You must,' Lucia insisted.

'I can't. I'm afraid I have to return to reality some time.'

'Don't be silly. Diego will never let you go.'

'He can't keep me here,' Maxie said gently.

'Don't you want to stay?'

Lucia looked so crushed that Maxie gave her a hug. 'Of course I do, but life doesn't always work out the way we want it to. That doesn't mean that you and I can't be friends.'

Lucia's warmth was something she couldn't bear to think of losing, any more than she could bear to think about leaving the only man she would ever feel she belonged with and this wild and beautiful land Diego called home.

'I think we should all do our best to change your mind,' Lucia said stubbornly, making a signal to her brothers that it was time for them to come in and eat supper. 'After all, you can work anywhere in the world, can't you?'

'Well, yes, as long as I'm free to travel. But—'

'No buts,' Lucia insisted. 'Don't you love Diego?'

Maxie paused. How could she possibly express her feelings for Diego? 'If only life could be more straightforward,' she said.

'It can be if you want it to be,' Lucia insisted. 'You have to fight for what you want, Maxie.'

Everything was black and white for Lucia, Maxie realised as the men cantered past and she exchanged a quick glance with Diego. She only wished she could share Lucia's innocent belief in the rightness of love and natural justice in life, but unlike her whimsical friend she was just too much the realist.

'With you at the helm, Holly's wedding is going to be a fabulous success,' Lucia enthused as they walked back to the house. 'I can't tell you how much we're all looking forward to it.'

'With your family in attendance, how can it be anything but a success?'

'Isla del Fuego *is* one of the most romantic places on earth,' Lucia said thoughtfully, 'but I would never get married anywhere but here on the *estancia* in Argentina.' Squeezing Maxie's arm again, she whispered in her ear, 'So I hope you're taking notes, my friend. Because I don't want anyone but you to arrange my wedding.'

Maxie laughed, glad at the change of subject. 'Do you have anyone in mind?'

'No, of course not,' Lucia protested.

But something in Lucia's eyes said yes, so Maxie

probed a little deeper. 'Tell me about the opposing polo team...'

'What do you want to know?' Lucia said defensively. 'Nero Caracas and his team are called The Assassins,' Lucia explained, but then her eyes narrowed and she drifted off into her own thoughts.

'Do you know the team well?' Maxie asked innocently.

Lucia's lips pressed down as she thought about it. 'Nero's gorgeous, of course, but he's off the market. He only got married recently, and he has a beautiful wife called Bella, as well as the most adorable baby girl called Natalia—Tally for short. I only know the rest of the team through my brothers—' Lucia stopped.

'And?' Maxie prompted, suspecting Lucia was holding something back.

'And they're all gorgeous, as well as the most amazing fun—except for one,' Lucia said frowning.

'And he is...?'

'Luke Forster—he flew over especially from America to play for Nero's Assassins. Don't know why they've asked *him* when there are so many perfectly good home-grown players here in Argentina.'

'Perhaps this Luke is better?' Maxie suggested tactfully.

Lucia huffed. 'He's supposed to be the best there is outside Argentina.'

'Well, there you are,' Maxie said soothingly. 'And I expect you'll tolerate his company somehow?'

'I suppose I'll have to,' Lucia agreed. 'But right now I'm more interested in you and Diego. You've done so much for him, Maxie. You can't walk out on him now.'

'I've no intention of walking out on him. Your brother has done more for me than you'll ever know.' He had allowed her to shake off the past and look forward to the future with confidence, Maxie mused as she stared at Diego, who was checking his pony's legs. Her heart rolled over when he glanced up. She had always known this affair must end, and that she and Diego led very different lives, but that didn't make it any easier.

So enjoy it while you can...

'I can't tell you what it means to Diego, having you here,' Lucia said, giving Maxie's arm a shake to bring her back from the daydream. 'And what you've done for our charity—what you've achieved in so short a time—is incredible. Especially when you've been finishing up Holly's wedding arrangements too.' Lucia shook her head as she waved her arm around to encompass all the colourful stalls decorated with bunting and flags, as well as the various groups of entertainers Maxie had imported from Buenos Aires in readiness for the great day. 'You're a marvel, Maxie.'

'As long as you and the family are happy with what I've arranged.'

'Happy?' Lucia squeezed Maxie's arm. 'I think you must know that's an understatement.'

It was one of those golden moments when she should feel nothing but happiness, Maxie realised, but instead she found herself wondering if she had ever been more on the outside looking in. For this world of staunch family loyalties and unshakeable togetherness was one she could never truly be part of.

CHAPTER TWELVE

LIFE was a game of snakes and ladders, Diego reflected as he showered after training. Even in his blackest and most despairing mood he had clung to that. When the doctors had told him he might never regain full use of his leg he had dared to believe he would play again. Then fate had brought him Maxie Parrish—a girl he'd be tempted to share everything with had it not been for all her secrets.

What about his?

He had never told anyone outside the family about Oresto. The shame he felt at having introduced his best friend to a low-life swindler had never left him. The consequences for Oresto had been catastrophic, and even now Diego realised, when he heard the three girls laughing uproariously in the kitchen, the shadow of Oresto's death could still fill him with niggling unease.

'Is everything ready for the match?' Maxie asked him brightly when he walked into the kitchen, her eyes sparkling as she came up to him.

Ruffling his hair, he dragged her into his arms and kissed her. That was his answer. It was the only answer that made any sense to him.

His impulse garnered lovestruck glances from both Holly and his sister, who quickly looked away. He saw them exchange knowing glances when he and Maxie pulled apart.

Would he ever get enough of her? Probably not, he thought as two of his brothers barged noisily into the kitchen. Maxie flashed an intimate glance at him before going over to them to discuss the arrangements she'd made for accommodating the stable lads who were flying to London with ponies they were exchanging with another breeder. He watched as she chatted easily with men whom most found intimidating. There was no denying she fitted right in.

The Acostas were a strong team, who supported each other through thick and thin. The fighter in him said that whatever secrets Maxie was hiding they could sort them out together. He had grown to care about her, and all that mattered to him was Maxie's happiness. She was unique. She was loyal. She got on with everyone. She made things run smoothly for the family. He could tell his brothers were as pleasantly surprised as he had been that on top of all her other responsibilities Maxie had managed to schedule the transportation of the ponies with the minimum of fuss and disruption on the day of the match.

'You're a fantastic organiser, Maxie,' observed his brother Kruz, who wasn't noted for giving out praise lightly.

'The addition of women into our wolves' den is a big plus, don't you think?' his brother Ruiz demanded, clapping Diego on the shoulder.

'At least I have some support, now Holly and Maxie are on my team,' Lucia put in.

'And at least we don't have to suffer Nacho's cooking,' Kruz added wryly.

'*You* cook if you don't like it,' his sister Lucia taunted, tossing a pack of steaks at Kruz, which he caught with a grin before heading outdoors to start the barbecue.

'What's all this?' Nacho growled, kicking his boots off at the door.

'We were just saying how much we love your cooking,' Lucia told him, with a wink in Maxie's direction.

Diego was content to soak all this in. He didn't know when he had ever seen the family so happy, or the dynamics of the group working so well. And a lot of that was due to Maxie, he realised as he pulled her into his arms. Maxie brought everyone together.

'This woman is very special to me,' he announced, never taking his gaze from Maxie's face.

'Like we don't know that,' Lucia exclaimed, hugging them both.

Did she dare to hope that this could last? Closing her eyes, Maxie wished she could stop time right here, right now. But time marched inexorably on.

The day of the match dawned bright and clear. The sense of excitement at the *estancia* was electric. Maxie had really pulled the stops out with the carnival, and the big house with its massive courtyard and formal gardens provided a perfect backdrop for the funfair in the field, the colourful stalls lined up in the home paddock, and the musicians warming up. The various bands were trying to outdo each other, but no one cared because this was fiesta, this was carnival. Everyone had made the effort to travel deep into the pampas—by jet, by helicopter, or by battered truck and motorbike. Some of the families arrived in horse-drawn carts piled high with their belongings for several nights' stay, and Maxie had organised the best of facilities for all of them to ensure that nothing could go wrong today.

* * *

He thought of Oresto a lot on the morning of a match. He always did. He wanted to tell Maxie how he thought about his friend each time he played, and how he felt guilty for enjoying the youth and life Oresto had lost. He wanted to tell her all of it before he cantered onto the field, because playing polo at this level was dangerous and he never knew what might happen—horses could suffer serious injury and riders had been killed. Did he want Maxie to find out about Oresto from anyone but him? What sort of a coward would that make him?

He brooded darkly on this as he went to make one last check on the ponies, but when Maxie waved to him on her way to the stands, arm in arm with his sister and Holly, he knew he couldn't mar her happiness with his memories. It was enough that she was here for him, on this the most important playing day of his life—his first day back after injury—the day when he must prove himself or withdraw from the game completely, for he would never let his brothers down.

He would speak to Maxie after the match, Diego determined. There were a lot of things he needed to straighten out with her. Working out a way for them to be together was top of his list. Maxie could continue her career anywhere in the world, so there was no reason why they couldn't be together. Smiling, he caught sight of her huddled in a giggling group with his sister and Holly, and it only confirmed his decision to can the last of his doubts and brush aside the black cloud of grief that always lodged over him before fire flashed through his veins when the match began. He couldn't interrupt the girls when he'd never seen Maxie so happy and relaxed.

Dios! The opposing team was on fire. Diego urged his mount into an even faster gallop. Nero Caracas in particular, along with his wing man, the American number one Luke Forster, were burning up the field. Their horses might as well have wings—they could turn a one-eighty in a heartbeat.

And Nero had his new wife to impress, Diego remembered, checking out Maxie in the stands as he galloped back to change his horse at the end of the second chukka. Just seeing her face reassured him that he had something important to fight for too.

I can't, Maxie had been about to say. But how could she say that? How could she even think it?

'Of course I'll leave immediately,' she confirmed, remembering the jet was fuelled and ready on the airstrip, waiting to take the exchange ponies to England. Fate could be kind sometimes, and at other times incredibly cruel. It was playing some hideous trick on her today by offering to be both.

'What's wrong?' Lucia demanded, sensing trouble.

'I have to leave immediately,' Maxie explained, texting furiously to make sure the flight didn't leave without her.

'You can't leave now!' Lucia exclaimed, grabbing her arm. 'Diego needs you here. They're losing the match, which means his chance to play again at international level is at risk. You can't walk out on him...'

Maxie saw her new friend's incredulity slowly turn to anger.

'I can't believe you'd do this to Diego,' Lucia said coldly.

She had to go. Maxie's father had suddenly taken a turn for the worst. And, as if that wasn't bad enough, a private investigator had been snooping round. Nothing else on earth could make her leave.

'Lucia, I must.'

'Must you?' Lucia said flatly, turning away.

All the warmth Maxie had felt at being welcomed into the heart of such a wonderful family turned to cold that invaded every part of her. So much so that when she stood to leave the stands—to leave Diego and the *estancia*. Argentina and the Acostas, without so much as a word of explanation to any of them—she was shivering violently beneath the fierce sun.

'Please tell Diego I love him…'

'Shouldn't you tell him that yourself?' Lucia demanded coldly.

'Please, Lucia.'

'Maxie, I'm struggling to understand this.'

'I wouldn't go if I didn't have to.' Sinking down in her seat again, conscious of precious seconds ticking by, she gripped Lucia's arm. 'Please don't think I'd do this if there was any other way.'

At first Lucia wouldn't look at her, but finally she relented. 'Can I do anything to help?'

Closing her eyes, Maxie tried not let emotion get the better of her. Lucia's big-hearted gesture was so typical of the whole Acosta family. 'I only wish you could, but this is something I have to do myself.' Embracing Diego's sister fiercely, she dashed away her tears and left the stand.

The first half had ended miserably for the Acostas. The team was down ten two. Diego was pacing impatiently, waiting for the grooms to bring up his next pony, when the call came through. It was his PI. For a moment he couldn't speak, he couldn't think.

Maxie was Peter Parrish's daughter?

The PI was at pains to explain that Maxie couldn't have been involved in the scam as she'd been too young.

His head was still reeling when he grabbed hold of

a groom. 'Tell them to hold the second half.' The man looked at him as if he'd gone mad. 'Tell them to wait for me,' he repeated as he sprinted for the stands.

Why hadn't she told him?

Fury coiled in his stomach like a venomous snake. He had brought Maxie into his family. He had trusted her. His could see the similarities now in the curve of her mouth and in a certain cadence in her voice. Peter Parrish had been a mesmerising charmer.

'Diego!'

He almost ran her over as she ran from the stands. He blocked her path so she had nowhere to go. He didn't speak. He didn't need to. She could see everything on his face.

'Diego, what is it? Did Lucia call you? Did she tell you I was leaving?'

'Leaving?' His phone buzzed imperatively. He ignored it. 'No one told me you were leaving. I had no idea.' He said this in the same chilling tone as his world disintegrated in front of his eyes. 'I came to see you—to speak to you—but now I find you're leaving in the middle of the match. Where are you going, Maxie?'

'To England. I have to—'

She was agitated and glanced at her watch, reminding him there was a flight to the UK waiting on the airstrip.

'I didn't want it to be like this, Diego.'

'How should it be?' he asked her in the same quiet voice. 'Were you just going to sneak away?'

'I need time to explain, Diego, and there is no time.' She glanced round, as if seeking the freedom he was denying her.

'This is one last chance for you to be honest with me.' His voice had hardened.

'What do you mean?' she said defensively. Her normally steady grey gaze was restless and distracted.

'Why are you leaving?' he demanded. 'What is so important it can't even wait until the end of the match? Who are you going to see, Maxie?'

Each second she remained silent marked a year since he had introduced his friend Oresto Fernandez to an unscrupulous crook named Peter Parrish. They had been young bloods in London, trying to prove themselves independently of their families. Diego's stake in what had turned out to be a scam had been small, just a trial to see how things worked out. He hadn't realised Oresto was gambling with family money. They had lost everything, and the friend he had grown up with and loved like a brother had hung himself in despair.

'Why are you looking at me like that, Diego?' she asked him fearfully.

As if he hated her? As if he hated everything surrounding Peter Parrish and anyone connected to him?

When tears of panic and bewilderment clouded Maxie's eyes he felt nothing. The crowd was already seated, waiting for the second half. A posse of grooms had just rounded the corner, searching for him.

'You have a decision to make,' he told Maxie coldly, turning away.

Diego's face was dark with fury. Maxie had chosen her father. The pilot of the jet had just called to confirm that she was safely on board. His brothers, seeing his expression, had begged him not to play.

'The match is going badly and the Acostas don't lose,' he told them. 'We do not play our greatest rivals at a charity match and canter off in front of our home crowd defeated and disgraced. That doesn't happen. It has never happened. And it won't happen today.'

'There are substitutes who can take your place,' his brother Nacho pointed out, pulling him away to clap a reassuring hand on Diego's shoulder.

'And risk my place in the national team?' Diego shook his head. 'You can rely on me, Nacho.' And for once even his formidable brother didn't argue with him.

He played like a man possessed. He took on the great Nero Caracas and nearly unseated him. It was said that when Diego Acosta played at his fiercest and most intimidating best the devil rode on his shoulder. Today he *was* the devil.

CHAPTER THIRTEEN

SHE was leaving her heart in Argentina, while duty and a very different type of love was taking her to England. It was too late to wish she had told Diego about her father. He couldn't have come with her anyway. And why would he want to? How could she be so selfish as to even think of asking him in the middle of a match that would decide Diego's future?

Even now she might arrive too late to find her father alive. With no one to see her she let the tears come as the powerful jet engines carried her swiftly above the cloud line and everything she had longed to be part of. She had to find the old, organised Maxie, who would immediately know what to do, but she was gone.

So she'd get her back, Maxie determined fiercely. First she had to prioritise. There would be other matches, but this visit with her father couldn't wait. She couldn't live with herself if she didn't go to him and he died alone.

And Diego?

She would call Diego the moment she arrived in London. She would tell him and he would understand. She *hoped* he would understand, Maxie amended as her heart contracted into a tiny, defensive ball.

* * *

Nacho's helicopter took Diego to Ezeiza International. From there the flight to London would take the same time as the jet. He was a mere six hours behind her. The trail was still hot.

His investigator was waiting for him at Heathrow with a fast, unobtrusive car. 'Move over, I'll drive,' he told the man. 'Just give me directions.'

And that was the extent of their conversation until he pulled in through the gates of the Nuttingford Nursing Home.

'What's this?' he said, peering out of the windscreen at the imposing Victorian façade. 'Has Peter Parrish taken to swindling old ladies these days?'

'It's a retirement home, for those who can afford it,' his investigator explained.

'Thank you.' He cut the man short. He could see for himself that there was everything here to make a con-man's twilight years extravagantly comfortable. Anger exploded inside him.

Peter Parrish was evidently prospering in this over-blown honeypot while Diego's friend Oresto was rotting in his grave. Spinning the car across the gravel, he screeched to a halt in front of the steps. Springing out, he slammed the door and took the steps in a couple of bounds. The front door was open and the PI followed him in. He was ready to do murder by the time he reached the reception desk, so perhaps it was as well that the investigator supplied the name under which Maxie had registered her father.

'You can leave me now,' he told the man, dismissing him without a glance.

He would confront Peter Parrish first, and then he would tell the world about a man without scruples so no one else would ever fall victim to his scams. If Maxie was with him... He steeled his heart. If Maxie was with her father she would have to admit her role in covering up his whereabouts and lying about his name. She must accept the full extent of her father's fraudulent dealings, together with their tragic consequences.

Guilt and anger vied inside him as he mounted the stairs, dragging on stale air at least five degrees warmer than it should have been. The thought of redemption and penance within his grasp drove him on. The upcoming confrontation wouldn't raise Oresto from the grave, but it would be the end of a journey he had once feared would never be over.

Stalking along a richly furnished corridor that boasted a faint scent of overcooked cabbage and beeswax, he found the room on the second floor. One of the better rooms, the receptionist had told him. As if he cared. As if he was interested in anything other than the fact that Peter Parrish had feathered his nest at the expense of who knew how many others apart from Oresto. He grasped the handle and threw the door open without the courtesy of a warning knock.

'Diego!'

'What the hell?' He whirled in turmoil before he had a chance to see inside the room, to find Maxie standing right behind him. His angry mind threw him back to the past even as he tried to absorb this new information.

She had just been coming out of the restroom when she spotted Diego. So he knew. He'd come. He was here for her. This was right. In that instant all the lonely sorrow banked up inside her changed to relief. He understood, she registered numbly as Diego steered her towards the empty visitors' lounge. When they were both inside he shut the door and leaned with his back against it so no one could disturb them.

'Well?' he said.

Oh, thank God to be with someone who understood

without the need for words. Diego's voice penetrated the mud in her head, just as the sight of him filled her heart with soothing balm. 'Oh, Diego…' She stopped. There was so much she wanted to say to him. 'Thank you for coming.' He made a sound, as if to say anything else was unthinkable. She could see the passion in his eyes—the fierce, fierce passion. 'I wish I could have waited for you. I wish I could have stayed to see the end of the match, but this…' Her hands lifted and fell again. There were no words.

'The match?' he said without inflection.

'I know how much it meant to you…' She lifted her gaze then, and stared him in the eyes.

'You had to be here,' he said in the same calm voice, his burning eyes the only reflection of the deepest of passions swirling inside him.

'Yes, I did. Thank you for understanding.'

The sound he made now was both primal and terrifying. *'Understanding?'* he spat out, grabbing hold of her. She cried out like a frightened animal when he yanked her close. Staring furiously into her eyes, he said, 'I only understand that you're here with *him.*'

'Yes, I know—I should have been with you.'

'Me?' he said, staring down at her as if she were his most loathsome enemy. 'You were *never* with me.'

'What are you saying?' Shock coursed through her even as bewilderment sapped the strength from her legs. 'Diego, I don't understand…'

'You don't understand?' he raged. 'You were always with *him*—calling him—speaking to him—thinking only of him.'

'Diego, please!'

He let her go as suddenly as he had grabbed hold of her and stood back, breathing heavily, lost in some place where she couldn't reach him. The world was going crazy. This wasn't her tender lover or the friend she had trusted above all others.

'Diego, what is it? Are you talking about my father? Are you jealous of my father? Diego?'

A discreet tap on the door made them both go still. Maxie's heart contracted. She knew what this meant.

'Diego,' she said softly. 'I have to go now.'

When she left him his fury subsided, leaving only the knowledge that he loved Maxie with all his heart, and that life without her was unthinkable. If she wanted to be with her father in private he would understand. He would be here for her, whatever happened. If Peter Parrish chose to ridicule and belittle him, then he would take that on board too. Love had no boundaries, no restrictions. Love was unconditional.

Walking over to the window, he stared out, remembering Oresto as the rain fell bleakly down.

The door to her father's room was partly open, and she heard the nurse outside explaining to Diego in an undertone, 'He doesn't have long. Please don't stay for more than a few minutes…'

The nurse's voice seemed to come from a long way away, while Maxie was in a bubble that excluded the rest of the world, apart from her father and now Diego. When the door swung wide to allow him in and she saw Diego framed in light calm fell over her, as if Diego being here at this particular time was part of the natural order of things. All the petty concerns and fears that jabbed away, making small problems seem huge, had been collected up in a holding pen to be dealt with at some later time. It was the only way individuals could cope with great grief, she supposed.

She heard Diego murmur something in reply to the nurse and then they were alone. Still holding her father's hand in both of hers, as if she could will some of her own strength into him, she turned to look at Diego.

Why hadn't she told him? He had remained in the visitors' lounge until he had begun to wonder if Maxie had left him again. He'd gone looking for her and a nurse had explained. And here she was, seated on an upright chair, holding the gnarled hand of the old man on the bed. His heart pounded with concern for her even as incredulity swept over him. Was *this* his enemy? Was *this* the man he had wasted so much of his life hating?

It took him a few moments to accept there could be any connection between the confident, robust individual he remembered and the frail old man who lay dying on the bed. The shades were drawn and there was no sound other than the ticking of an antique mantel clock and the old man's involuntary breathing. Peter Parrish had passed to the last struggles of a body ready to surrender, and while Maxie appeared resigned to this, he could feel her anguish and her deep sense of impending loss.

'Diego,' she whispered, reaching for him.

Taking hold of Maxie's hand in a firm grip, he raised it to his lips and pressed a long kiss against her palm. Only then did he straighten up to stare down at Peter Parrish. So this was the devil on his back. This was the man who had haunted him. How sweet were those thoughts of revenge now?

'I'm so glad you're here,' Maxie whispered.

He stared down into her eyes and saw only goodness in them. Maxie had never been to blame for her father's actions. She hadn't been hiding wickedness from him—she had been hiding love. Peter Parrish might be undeserving of that love but he was Maxie's father. And if there was one thing Diego understood it was family. There was only one thing he could do now, and that was to forgive Peter Parrish as Oresto's family had forgiven him.

Diego reflected as he watched her moisten her father's lips with a sponge left for that purpose. This was life. This was Maxie's life. A great shame washed over him when he thought how badly he had misjudged her. He hadn't really let her in. If he had he would have told her about Oresto and she would have been able to confide in him about her father.

'I would have left the match to be with you,' he whispered.

'I couldn't have asked you to do that,' she protested in an undertone. 'Your first match back, Diego? Don't you think I know how important that was for you?'

He shrugged this off with a rueful breath. 'I'm just another player. There are always substitutes standing ready, longing for the chance to prove what they can do. You should have told me what was happening, Maxie. I would have brought you here.'

'I never thought you'd want that level of commitment.'

'What are you talking about?' he demanded incredulously, drawing her away from the bed to an alcove, where they could talk without disturbing her father.

'I've seen what love can do, Diego. I know how destructive it can be.'

She glanced at her father as she spoke, and it killed him to see her wringing her hands. Capturing them in his he held them safe as Maxie told him how her father had mistreated her mother and how he'd later been eaten up with guilt when her mother had become ill.

'But the guilt was too late,' she said. 'Just as it's too late for me to tell my father that I love him.'

'It's never too late,' he argued fiercely, dragging her close. 'You're here now, and I think your father knows that. I think he knows you've always been here for him, and that your forgiveness for whatever he's done in the past is limitless and was never in doubt.'

'Do you really think so?' she said, searching his face.

'I know it,' he ground out fiercely, holding her tight. 'I know it just as surely as I know that love can last. I know it in the same way that I know I can't live without you. Can you ever forgive me for not being here for you—for not telling you how I feel about you before this?'

'For not expressing your emotions?' She smiled sadly. 'Diego, we're both lousy at that.'

'So if I tell you I love you?'

The tension in her face softened. 'I never thought of you as a romantic, Diego.'

'And I never took you for a coward, Maxie Parrish. I still don't. So if I ask you to marry me, will you risk it?'

'Just hold me,' she begged him, nestling close. 'For now, just hold me.'

They stood for a long time without speaking, and when he released her she turned back to her vigil. He caught her before she reached the bed. 'I'll take over,' he said quietly. 'Please… Let me do this for you, Maxie.'

She looked at him in bewilderment.

'You need a break,' he said, appealing to her common sense. 'Sit down for a moment outside and gather your strength. I'll call you right away if you're needed.'

'I can't believe you'd do this for me.'

'I'd do anything for you,' he said simply. When she rested against him he felt how exhausted she was, and he knew he wouldn't tell her the history he shared with her father now. He wouldn't tell her for a long time, and only then if he thought she was ready to hear it—so maybe never. The only thing that mattered to him was caring for Maxie and supporting her when she needed him, and he thanked God for giving him this opportunity.

When they left the nursing home he realised Peter Parrish had taught him a valuable lesson. While he had been sitting with Maxie's father, doing all he could to make the man comfortable in the last hours of his life, he had taken the opportunity to review his own life, and had realised that the only thing that mattered was love.

'I should have told you about my father long before this,' Maxie said, worrying her lip as she frowned.

'No, you shouldn't.'

He was holding her in his arms on the bed at the *palacio* on the Isla del Fuego, where they were staying for Holly's wedding. They hadn't talked about Maxie's father since the funeral, when Diego had said a few words over the grave about forgiveness and redemption and moving on. Maxie was still tender after her father's death and needed constant reassurance. She had been holding it together for so long she hardly knew how to let go. He understood how vulnerable a strong person could be, and his heart had gathered her in.

'Why are you telling me all this now?' he said, kissing her brow.

'Because I want to share everything with you,' she said, turning her clear gaze on him. 'I don't want there to be any secrets between us.'

'And there won't be,' he pledged, dropping a tender kiss on her lips.

This return to Isla del Fuego, where they had first met,

first kissed, first argued, first loved, had been a poignant homecoming for both of them. He would always remember what Maxie had done for him here, as well as what she had created for Holly's wedding—scenes of such celebration and love that the old house and the island on which it stood had been reinstated in his memory as a happy place rather than a prison.

'Have I thought of everything?' she murmured, worrying because today was the long-awaited day of Holly's wedding.

'You know you have,' he reassured her, drawing Maxie into his arms.

The guests had been brought in by ferries which had been met on the dock by fleets of horse-drawn carriages, specially decorated with ribbons and flowers for the occasion. The weather, unlike on Maxie's first sighting of the island, couldn't have been more perfect, and everyone had enthused that this was going to be a wedding like no other. Even his hard to please brother Ruiz was in a perpetual state of ecstasy at the sight of the joy and anticipation on Holly's face.

And now he and Maxie were resting on the bed after the final dress rehearsal. The sex was always phenomenal between them, but just lying together quietly was good too. 'So, come on,' he coaxed, 'tell me what's on your mind.'

'I want to tell you everything,' she murmured against his mouth. 'Then we needn't speak of it again. But there is something I want you to know.'

'If it's worrying you, and it will make you feel better if you tell me, then do so,' he said. He would do anything to make Maxie happy.

'My father didn't always tread a straight line.'

His impulse was to tense. He caught it in time.

'But there was a reason for it,' she continued. 'When

my mother became sick we had no money for her care. That was when I learned how to massage her leg, because it saved paying for extra sessions from the therapist. I soon became good at it.'

'Because it mattered to you?' he guessed.

She smiled sadly. 'Because it helped my mother.'

He gave an encouraging nod.

'My father couldn't afford the treatment my mother needed,' she went on, 'and so he started to borrow money—more and more money.'

A downward spiral that had ended with Peter Parrish trying to swindle two cocky Argentinian youths out of a fortune, Diego realised.

'He wasn't a bad man, Diego. He was a desperate man. The money wasn't for him, but for my mother.'

He hushed her and drew her close to kiss the top of her head, thinking this hardly mattered now. But Maxie tensed and pulled away, her eyes full of some unspoken horror.

'What is it?' he said.

'It went wrong, Diego,' she said, staring at him with that same look in her eyes. 'My father's plan went horribly wrong. Someone died because of him. I was too young to know the details, but I heard my mother crying one day as she confided in a friend that a young man had lost all his family money and killed himself because of my father's actions. There were more rows, and my father was never the same after that. His intention, foolish though it was, had been to save life—not to destroy it. I think he went mad with grief, and then dementia took over. My mother died shortly afterwards, so he felt it had all been for nothing.'

'But none of it was your fault, Maxie,' Diego insisted gently. 'You can't go on blaming yourself for something

your father did so long ago. And you mustn't,' he insisted. 'Your father was trying in every way he knew
to care for your mother, as you later cared for him. He
could see no further than that any more than you could
see further than your duty towards him. Don't you think
I understand that now?'

Her eyes slowly cleared. 'You do, don't you?'

Maxie had taught him that love came at a cost, and
that sometimes that cost was high. She had been right
to defend her father. It was not right that Diego had allowed thoughts of revenge and rage to rampage through
him for so many wasted years, or that he had allowed
that fury onto the polo field, where it had nearly killed
him and his horse, and had made him a danger to every
other player in the game. He kissed her again to confirm
in his own mind that all that was behind him now. She
tasted so good, so sweet and fresh…so different, somehow.

What was different?

Some primal memory stirred inside him. 'Why are
you telling me this now?' he repeated gently, moving his
head on the pillow so she had to look at him.

'Because it's more important than ever that you and I
don't have any secrets between us,' she said, holding his
gaze trustingly.

He looked at her, frowning slightly. 'Why more important than ever?'

'Because we're going to have a baby, Diego.' She
stopped and bit down on her lip, as if she wasn't sure if
he'd be pleased.

He shot up in bed. 'Are you sure?'

'I'm positive,' she said quietly.

He exclaimed with pleasure—anticipation—excite-

ment—a world of emotion flashing behind his eyes. 'Can
we tell everyone?' he exulted.

'No, it's too soon. And the timing could be better.'

'How could it be better?' he demanded. 'The timing
is perfect,' he argued fiercely.

'Beating the bride to getting pregnant isn't so great—
especially when you're a wedding planner who is supposed to be so organised.'

'Nonsense!' he exclaimed. 'You got it exactly right—
for us.' Dragging her into his arms, he gazed into Maxie's
eyes intently, as if he would see some change there too.
'All right. I won't tell anyone,' he promised. 'At least not
today. You're going to be a mother!' he exclaimed softly
in wonder.

'And you're going to be a father,' Maxie agreed wryly.
'How do you feel about that, Diego?'

'How do I feel?' he demanded incredulously. 'As if
the world and everything in it is mine.'

'Diego,' she murmured when they finally found the
willpower to break apart, 'we've got a wedding to go to.'

Picking his watch up from the bedside table and glancing at it, he raised a brow.

'You are impossible,' she breathed as he pressed her
down on the bed.

'And you are the wholly irresistible mother of my
child,' he said, starting to unfasten the buttons on her
blouse.

He had made love to Maxie in the way he intended to
live his life from now on, Diego reflected as he exam-
ined his unusually smooth, freshly shaved face just before the wedding. Taking her gently and with reverence,
he had experienced a deep calm and certainty inside
him as she sighed with pleasure in his arms. She was

the mother of his child, and they had a lifetime ahead of them in which he intended to demonstrate his love for Maxie in so many ways—not all of them calm and with reverence, he amended, smiling to himself as he racked his brain for ways they hadn't made love yet.

'You look fantastic, Diego.'

He turned to find her standing in the doorway. Tousled and sexily sated, she looked fantastic too, wearing nothing more than a sheet. 'You'd better get a move on,' he told her.

'Don't I know it?' she agreed. 'But it won't take me long to shower and dress.'

She looked him over again. Diego was Ruiz's best man, and Holly had requested he wear a pale, lightweight linen suit with a white open-necked shirt and a vibrant orchid in his buttonhole to pick up the colour of the bridesmaids' dresses. Maxie adjusted his collar at the back, and then passed him some cologne which he slapped on reluctantly.

'Are you sure you like this?' he demanded, grimacing.

Maxie grinned. 'I like everything about you.'

'Later,' he murmured, teasing her as he comforted himself that they had all the time in the world now and that nothing could ever part them again. 'You'd better get ready,' he urged, dropping a kiss on the top of her head. 'You're the one person who can't afford to be late today. And I don't want Holly coming after me for distracting her wedding planner.'

'She'd be jealous if she knew the reason,' Maxie teased him.

'Not after tonight, I'm guessing,' Diego told her dryly, on his way out of the room.

Maxie would be in the background today, making sure

all her arrangements ran like clockwork. Her outfit would consist of a businesslike white shirt tucked into cream linen trousers, her only adornment the radio earpiece with attached microphone which she used to co-ordinate the various stages of the celebration.

'Quick shower, and then I'll see you downstairs,' she shouted after him.

'See you down there,' he confirmed from the door. He was heading for Ruiz and patted his pocket to make sure he had the ring. 'I love you,' he murmured, holding Maxie's gaze for one long, lingering moment.

CHAPTER FOURTEEN

EVEN Maxie was blown away by the scene she had helped to design. The vast courtyard was dressed with a profusion of colourful blossom, while the wedding arbour where the couple would exchange their vows was a fragrant mass of lush white flowers and soft green foliage. Gilt chairs with the palest gold seat pads were lined up either side of the pastel primrose carpet down which the bride would glide.

Having checked with her assistants that there was nothing more she could do for now, she ran up to the terrace at the top of the steps and watched the remaining guests taking their seats. The air of anticipation was electric. An orchestra was setting the scene with an elegant Bach concerto while people chatted easily to each other. This was the moment she always enjoyed. She had done everything possible to make a perfect day for the bride, and now it only remained for the main players to take the stage.

A fanfare announced the arrival of Ruiz, accompanied by his equally striking brother Diego. A rustle of excitement swept the crowd as they walked down the bridal carpet, stopping from time to time to greet friends. It looked like a scene from a fairytale, she thought as Diego turned to look at her. She shared a brief look, and then got back on her radio to let everyone know the groom and best man were in position. It was only when she had finished the call that she spotted trouble brewing.

All the guests were looking forward, towards the arbour where Ruiz and Diego were standing, but one elderly woman was staring back at Maxie. She didn't look like the usual troublemaker—someone who might have had too much to drink—this was a small, inoffensive-looking woman with neat grey hair. But the man seated at her side *did* look like trouble, and as he turned to stare Maxie was shocked to see the look he gave her. She couldn't imagine what she'd done to deserve it. It was obviously a case of mistaken identity. But the man was on his feet now, with the older woman hanging on to his wrist.

'Hold the bride,' Maxie rapped into her radio mike. 'I need a good ten to fifteen minutes here.'

A second call to the leader of the orchestra had them breaking into a jolly piece and playing much louder than they had before. The chattering guests were none the wiser, Maxie confirmed with relief. If words were to be exchanged this could be done discreetly now. She also warned Diego of a slight delay, taking care to make nothing of it. A last call to Lucia worked in her favour.

'I'm not ready yet,' Holly yelled in the background, and, seizing the receiver from Lucia, added, 'Haven't you heard of the bride's right to keep the groom waiting?'

'No, I never heard that before,' Maxie said, forcing a wry note into her voice. Cutting the line, she hurried down the steps to what was looking more like trouble with every passing second.

She spoke to the man first. 'Can I help you?'

She backed away as he came after her, with the older woman, Maxie presumed his mother, hot on his heels.

She wasn't running away from either of them. She was drawing them out of earshot of the other guests. Leading them behind a screen that divided the wedding congregation from the linen-draped tables where the drinks for the champagne reception were sitting. She asked politely once again what was wrong.

'You don't know me,' the man rapped with an ugly expression. 'But I know you.'

He came towards her, with his mother hanging on to his arm.

'My name is Maxie Parrish,' Maxie said evenly. 'I'm Holly's wedding planner. If I can help you in any way…?' Her voice might sound calm, but her heart was thundering at the sight of so much barely contained anger.

'My name is Alessandro Fernandez,' the man snarled, as if this should mean something to her. 'And this is my mother, Señora Fernandez.'

'I'm very pleased to meet you, Señora Fernandez,' Maxie said politely, extending her hand. Instead of shaking it, the old lady started to cry. 'Your mother's upset,' she exclaimed, when Alessandro took another menacing step towards her. Walking between him and his mother, she ushered Señora Fernandez towards one of the chairs set out for the older guests—and gasped with fright when Alessandro tried to grapple it from her.

'Alesssandro!' Señora Fernandez exclaimed, equally shocked.

Diego erupted round the screen, flinging himself between Maxie and Alessandro. It took all three of his brothers to hold him back. Flinging the chair aside with a roar of fury, Alessandro squared up to Diego, at which point Señora Fernandez entered the fray.

Maxie's first impulse was to shield the older woman. 'Can't you see you're upsetting your mother?'

'*I'm* upsetting her?' Alessandro ground out. 'I think

you will find it is you, Señorita Parrish, who insults my mother with your very presence at this wedding!'

'I'm the wedding planner,' Maxie pointed out. 'Why would I not be here? And how have I upset you?' Something made her look at Diego for the answer.

Before anyone had a chance to speak Alessandro's mother stepped in. 'This behaviour does you no credit, Alessandro. It will not bring your brother back.' Turning to Maxie, she added, 'Why is it only women who understand?'

The older woman's voice was tinged with such sadness that Maxie shot another look at Diego, but he was pinning Alessandro to the spot with a warning stare. She didn't know anyone in Argentina, Maxie reasoned. What could she possibly have done to have caused such distress?

'Alessandro.' Diego's voice was low and menacing. 'Your mother is right. This does no good.'

'And what do *you* know?' Alessandro sneered. 'You have no heart. You have no feelings. You're not capable of feeling anything, Diego. Does this woman know that?' he said, sparing a withering glance for Maxie.

'Alessandro!' Señora Fernandez exclaimed, her voice pure steel. 'Have you forgotten yourself entirely? Apologise to Señorita Parrish this instant, and keep your rough house behaviour for the polo field where your aggression can be safely channelled.'

If all these fierce-looking men were encouraged by their mothers to work off their aggression on the polo field no wonder they couldn't be beaten, Maxie reflected as Diego stepped forward.

'Señora,' he said with a courteous bow to Alessandro's mother, 'may I offer you a refreshing drink before we return to our seats?'

But Alessandro wasn't finished yet. 'How could you allow this woman to come here?' he hissed, staring at Maxie as his mother graciously accepted Diego's offer.

'Not now, Alessandro,' Diego warned, conscious of Maxie standing behind him in a state of bewilderment. Alessandro's expression of fury was nothing to the hurt he could see on Maxie's face, which seemed to say, *What haven't you told me?*

'Will everyone please take their places?' she said in a calm voice. 'Ruiz?' she prompted, escorting the groom towards the screen behind which his guests sat waiting. 'You wouldn't want Holly to be upset by any further delay, would you?'

Ruiz was instantly in the moment. 'Of course not,' he said, heading off.

'Diego, Nacho, Kruz,' she added firmly. 'Please go with your brother.'

'And leave you here?' Diego demanded, as his brothers peeled away.

Holly was issuing instructions over her radio, and it was Señora Fernandez who took the floor. 'Please remember this is a public occasion,' she told her son. 'If you care anything about family pride, as you say you do, then this is your chance to prove it.'

'Gracias, señora,' Maxie said gratefully as the men finally left the two women together. 'I don't understand what provoked this, but perhaps you and I can talk after the wedding?'

'I would like that,' Señora Fernandez agreed.

Having restarted the programme for the day, Maxie thanked Señora Fernandez again for her intervention.

'You were doing very well on your own,' Señora Fernandez insisted. 'You seem to have a talent for handling hotheads,' she added wryly.

There was iron in that voice, but also sadness, Maxie thought as the older woman reached out to touch her face. 'Let's go,' Señora Fernandez announced, heading for the screen. 'We have a wedding to celebrate, don't we, Maxie?'

'Yes, we do,' Maxie agreed, hoping she'd stop shaking soon as she gave the go-ahead to the bride.

He had thought he'd lost everything after the accident, but that had been nothing compared to this, Diego realised. Getting through the wedding with good grace was the hardest thing he had ever had to do. He hadn't had a chance to explain what had happened to Maxie, and now he wondered if he was about to lose everything he cared about. He had tried to draw Maxie's attention during the long day, but she was always busy and there had been no chance for a private word. But every second he left her bewildered about what had happened was too long, and he had his speech to make yet.

Was it only she who was in the dark? The wedding ran as if on oiled wheels, but there was no chance to ask Diego about the heated exchange as Maxie would be on duty until the last guest went to bed.

She insisted on staying until everything had been cleared away, and Diego came looking for her to remind her that she had a baby to think of now.

'I wanted to speak to Señora Fernandez before I turned in.' She snatched a glance at her watch and grimaced when she saw the time.

'Señora Fernandez will be fast asleep by now,' Diego confirmed. 'You should be too.'

'What was that about, Diego?'

'I'll answer questions tomorrow.'

'No. Tonight,' Maxie insisted as all the hurt and bewilderment welled up inside her. 'We promised we'd share everything,' she reminded him.

'And I will.'

'Now, Diego.'

He took her to the stables, and they walked down the line of stalls where horses were breathing softly. 'You never did tell me who won the polo match,' she said.

'Does it matter?'

'You scored the winning goal.'

'Lucia told you? All I could think of was getting back to you. I just wanted the match over with. The only irony was winning my place back on the team when I thought I'd lost everything.'

'And today at the wedding?' she prompted. 'Why does Alessandro hate me so much, Diego? I don't even know him.'

Opening a door onto the hay barn, he took her inside. 'This is where I come when I have something on my mind,' he said. 'The horses are good company.'

'You mean they don't answer back?' Maxie suggested wryly.

Diego huffed a laugh. Shrugging off his jacket, he tossed it on a bale of hay and brought her down with him. 'Señora Fernandez and Alessandro are my best friend Oresto's mother and brother. Many years ago Oresto met a man who promised him he could change his life. That man was your father...'

Maxie drew in a sharp breath. 'Diego...?'

'I introduced them, and together we thought we could make lots of money. But sadly this story does not have a happy ending. I think you know how it ends...'

'The boy who killed himself?' Maxie exclaimed softly.

'Now it all makes sense. That lovely woman—Diego, I can't bear it. No wonder Alessandro was so angry when he realised who I was.'

'We can't change the past, but we can learn from it. I've laid my ghosts, Maxie. It's time for you to do the same.'

'I can't believe you were so closely associated with my father all those years ago. It's incredible to imagine it.'

'Our lives were intertwined before we even knew it,' he murmured, kissing her brow.

'What a tragedy,' she whispered, shifting restlessly in his arms. 'I can understand why Alessandro hates me.'

'Alessandro doesn't hate you. He will see sense and calm down. He always does.'

'But Señora Fernandez—'

'—is a very special woman. She forgave me many years ago. She told me that no more young lives should be wasted because of money. And I think she likes you.'

'I hope so,' Maxie murmured, relaxing.

'I repaid all the money Oresto lost—with interest.'

'And my father?'

Diego would never speak ill of the dead, let alone re-mind Maxie of a bad time in her life. 'I learned a lot from your father,' he said honestly.

'About what not to do?' she suggested.

His answer was to kiss her, and when he released her he said, 'I'll do everything in my power to keep you safe and prove that love can last, that it can become stronger with each passing year.'

Reassured, she snuggled close—and was so exhausted she slept until dawn.

'So, what shall we do now?' he said, turning to look at her as she stirred sleepily.

'I don't know,' she admitted. 'Have you got any ideas?'

'I've got a few,' he said.

It was three months later when Diego led Maxie through the doors of a prominent London store. They were staying with Ruiz and Holly in their London home, and making the most of all the wonderful shopping opportunities.

'What are we doing here?' Maxie demanded. 'The store is closing, Diego.'

'Not for you,' he said, steering her towards the elevator.

Not for Diego Acosta, Maxie amended wryly as a uniformed security guard personally escorted them in the opposite direction to the crowds heading home. She was touched to find Diego was taking her to the floor that specialised in nursery equipment.

'This is where you get to pick what you want and I get to pick what I want,' he explained.

'So, what do *you* want?' she said, frowning as she gazed down the aisles packed with baby equipment. 'I don't even know where to start—there's so much to choose from!'

'True,' Diego agreed. 'But I've already made my choice. If you'll have me, Maxie…?'

'Are you serious?'

'I'm down on one knee in front of witnesses. Will you marry me, Señorita Parrish? I should warn you before you answer there is one condition.'

'Which is?'

'You find another wedding planner to arrange our big day.'

After choosing the equipment for their first child's nursery, he took Maxie to a fairground. He wanted her to have something frivolous and fun to remember the day by, and he locked that memory in with a rather serious diamond ring. Maxie could run a business for as long as she wanted, but when they were together he wanted both of them to make time to have fun together—fun was something that had been conspicuous by its absence in Maxie's life before they met, as far as he could gather. 'I love you, Señora Acosta-to-be,' he told her as the big wheel soared into the sky.

'And I love you too, *señor*,' she told him, snuggling close. 'More than you will ever know.'

'Show me that ring,' he teased her.

She held up her hand to admire it.

It would take many years of persuasion before Maxie would believe that he *hadn't* arranged fireworks to choose that precise moment to light up the sky.

EPILOGUE

MAXIE'S wedding dress was the most feminine thing she had ever worn. A simple column of ivory silk, overlaid with the most exquisite cobweb-fine Swiss lace, skimmed her body to her hips before flaring into a fuller skirt with a filmy lace train. She held a modest trailing bouquet of blush pink peonies and fragrant white freesia, interspersed with the palest green feathery foliage. Lucia and Holly were her attendants, and there was one very special page boy—a six-month-old baby boy. Though Jaime Acosta slept peacefully throughout the ceremony in Señora Fernandez's arms.

Needless to say Jaime already had his first pony. Diego had picked out a small grey for his son within an hour of his birth. Diego might be a little crazy, and Maxie was definitely the person people came to when they wanted something sorted out, but Maxie thought that was why it worked so well between them: they were like two pieces of a jigsaw that fitted perfectly together.

'Ready?' Lucia demanded in a voice full of suppressed excitement as she carefully handed Maxie down from the horse-drawn carriage outside the tiny chapel at the *estancia*.

'For anything,' Maxie agreed, squeezing Lucia's hand.

'That's just as well,' Holly agreed wryly.

'You look beautiful,' Señora Fernandez exclaimed—sentiments that were echoed by the housekeepers, Maria and Adriana.

'Thank you,' Maxie whispered, kissing each of the older women on the cheek in turn, before dropping a kiss on her son's downy brow.

'I'm so happy for you,' Holly exclaimed, tweaking Maxie's veil. 'Wait until Diego sees you!'

Maxie had to admit it was quite a transformation from the bedraggled girl who had arrived on a tiny island in the middle of a storm with only business on her mind.

Had she really thought she was ready for this?

When Diego turned to look at her as she entered the chapel the breath left Maxie's chest in a rush. She hardly remembered the ceremony, but when they came out to the cheers of their guests as man and wife she did remember the look she had shared with Diego throughout, the silent pledge that bound them for life. And with the blessings and goodwill of everyone around them there was only one duty left for the bride...

'Oh, *no!*' Lucia exclaimed as she caught Maxie's bouquet.

As if Lucia hadn't batted every other woman out of the way in order to leap up and snatch it for herself, Maxie thought, laughing as she turned around. 'You can always give it back to me and I'll throw it again,' she suggested.

'No way,' Lucia replied, to groans of complaint from the other women. 'These flowers need water,' she explained briskly, as a certain American polo player hoved into view.

Then Diego was at Maxie's side, with their son in his arms. 'The jet is waiting,' he murmured discreetly. 'Can we leave now? I can't wait to have you on my own.'

'I love you,' Maxie whispered, staring deep into her husband's eyes. 'I love you both so much.'

'You've given me more than you know,' Diego said, putting a protective arm around her shoulders, 'and my love for you grows stronger every day.'

* * * * *

A sneaky peek at next month...

MODERN™

INTERNATIONAL AFFAIRS, SEDUCTION & PASSION GUARANTEED

My wish list for next month's titles...

In stores from 16th March 2012:

❏ A Deal at the Altar — Lynne Graham

❏ Gianni's Pride — Kim Lawrence

❏ The Legend of de Marco — Abby Green

❏ Deserving of His Diamonds? — Melanie Milburne

In stores from 6th April 2012:

❏ Return of the Moralis Wife — Jacqueline Baird

❏ Undone by His Touch — Annie West

❏ Stepping out of the Shadows — Robyn Donald

❏ Girl Behind the Scandalous Reputation — Michelle Conder

❏ Redemption of a Hollywood Starlet — Kimberly Lang

Available at WHSmith, Tesco, Asda, Eason, Amazon and Apple

Just can't wait?

Visit us Online

You can buy our books online a month before they hit the shops! **www.millsandboon.co.uk**

0312/01

Book of the Month

MICHELLE CONDER
Girl Behind the Scandalous Reputation

We love this book because...

Hollywood starlet Lily Wild is caught in a scandal that has every paparazzi flashbulb exploding! Her only escape is world-class lawyer Tristan Garrett—a man convinced of her guilt! Michelle Conder's feisty, sexy debut is strikingly contemporary and utterly unmissable!

On sale 6th April

Visit us Online

Find out more at
www.millsandboon.co.uk/BOTM

0312/BOTM

MILLS & BOON Book Club

Save over £40

Join the Mills & Boon Book Club

Subscribe to **Modern**™ today for 3, 6 or 12 months and you could **save over £40!**

We'll also treat you to these fabulous extras:

- **FREE L'Occitane gift set** worth £10
- **FREE home delivery**
- Books up to 2 months ahead of the shops
- Bonus books, exclusive offers… and much more!

Subscribe now at
www.millsandboon.co.uk/subscribeme

Visit us Online

Save over £40 – find out more at **www.millsandboon.co.uk/subscribeme**

SUBS/OFFER/P

Special Offers

Every month we put together collections and longer reads written by your favourite authors.

Here are some of next month's highlights— and don't miss our fabulous discount online!

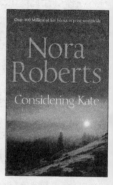

On sale 16th March

On sale 16th March

On sale 6th April

Save 20%
on all Special Releases

Find out more at
www.millsandboon.co.uk/specialreleases

Visit us Online

0312/ST/MB364

Mills & Boon® Online

Discover more romance at
www.millsandboon.co.uk

- 🌹 **FREE** online reads
- 🌹 **Books** up to one month before shops
- 🌹 **Browse our books** before you buy

...and much more!

For exclusive competitions and instant updates:

 Like us on **facebook.com/romancehq**

 Follow us on **twitter.com/millsandboonuk**

 Join us on **community.millsandboon.co.uk**

Visit us Online

Sign up for our FREE eNewsletter at
www.millsandboon.co.uk

WEB/M&B/RTL4

The World of Mills & Boon®

There's a Mills & Boon® series that's perfect for you. We publish ten series and with new titles every month, you never have to wait long for your favourite to come along.

Blaze®   Scorching hot,
                 sexy reads

By Request   Relive the romance with
                 the best of the best

Cherish™   Romance to melt the
                 heart every time

Desire™   Passionate and dramatic
                 love stories

Visit us Online   Browse our books before you buy online at
                    www.millsandboon.co.uk

M&B/WORLD

What will you treat yourself to next?

Ignite your imagination, step into the past...

INTRIGUE... Breathtaking romantic suspense

Medical Romance Captivating medical drama—with heart

MODERN™ International affairs, seduction and passion

nocturne™ Deliciously wicked paranormal romance

RIVA™ Live life to the full – give in to temptation

You can also buy Mills & Boon eBooks at
www.millsandboon.co.uk

Visit us Online

M&B/WORLD

B

Have Your Say

You've just finished your book.
So what did you think?

We'd love to hear your thoughts on our
'Have your say' online panel
www.millsandboon.co.uk/haveyoursay

- 🌹 Easy to use
- 🌹 Short questionnaire
- 🌹 Chance to win Mills & Boon® goodies

Visit us Online

Tell us what you thought of this book now at
www.millsandboon.co.uk/haveyoursay

YOUR_SAY